The Healer

Seven Sins MC #2

—

Jessica Gadziala

DEDICATION

To everyone who read, loved, and demanded more
from this world.
You guys just continue to make dreams come true.

Chapter One

The scream tore through the canyon, echoing back the same ear-splitting sound, but hollowing it out, intensifying it.

It was a familiar sound.

A *hellish* sound.

I tried not to let any sort of hope swell. We'd been through this half a dozen times for the past year with no results.

None of the spots ended up having enough energy left in them for Lenore to open up the Hellmouths like she'd been able to once before.

The night we lost Red and somehow got stuck with the demon version of a puppy and his curmudgeonly older brother.

Since then, though, nothing.

We'd traveled across the country, up into Canada, down into Mexico. And while Lenore claimed each of the spots had the right energy she could sense, none of the spells she'd tried could break through the earth, open up way down into the depths of hell.

So there we all were, standing in a deep canyon in Utah in the middle of the fucking winter. No amount of moving around, or layers of clothing seemed like they could chase the chill away. It had burrowed through my skin, muscles, organs, and was deep in my marrow, a constant and distracting sensation.

"Keep going," I demanded, getting a hard look from Lycus, not liking it when he thought I was getting pushy with his woman.

The ground trembled beneath our feet, a small hole emerging a few feet in front of Lenore, the earth crumbling down inside as the heat rose up. I only barely resisted the urge to place my hands over it, warming them like one might with a campfire.

Minos stood back from our gathered circle, knowing there was no way for him to go back, that he was stuck on the human plane for eternity, never dying, never getting a break from his misery.

That was part of the reason we needed to get back so badly. I'd already lost two of my men to the Claiming. I couldn't afford to lose Aram, Seven, Drex, and now Daemon and Bael.

It seemed like the longer we were on Earth, the more susceptible we became to pesky human needs and desires.

None of us ever could have known that, prepared for it, since there had never been any records of demons leaving hell and getting stuck in the human world for as long as we had. Or if anyone had, they'd never made it back to hell to tell their stories.

Who knew what the fuck could happen to us if we stayed another hundred years. Two hundred.

We had to get back.

I'd made peace with the idea of leaving Minos, of leaving Ly. Even if doing so made me feel like a failure as a leader. It was my place to guide them, to teach them, to protect them if necessary.

I'd failed.

I hadn't had the knowledge.

And they would suffer for it, staying here in this dumpster fire of a world while the rest of us went home, got to get back to work, continued to fulfill the lifestyles we were made for.

Fire and brimstone and all that.

Anticipation skittered over my nerve endings, giving me temporary relief from the cold that clung to me like death, its cold fingers raking its long nails over every inch of skin no matter how many layers I piled on, how warm we kept the heat.

"I like it here," I heard Daemon complain under his breath. Young and stupid, he thought his destiny was between the thighs of a human woman, so he buried himself between as many as possible.

"Shut the fuck up," Bael, his older brother growled, positioning himself slightly behind his younger brother's shoulder in case he got any ideas about running off, trying to stay here.

"Get back," Lenore said, voice a little tight as she herself moved back several feet as the ground kept falling inward, as the heat got more intense.

It was the most comfortable I'd felt in a year and a half. Since the last time Lenore had been able to open a Hellmouth. And not just because of the comforting warmth. But the promise of getting back to where we were always meant to be, doing what we were meant to do.

Sure, we kept ourselves busy here.

We had house parties and went to rallies. We passed around drugs and our bodies and our voices, whispering encouragement to the humans, bringing out their innate, often barely-buried evils.

The fire always needed fuel and we'd been feeding the flames for generations.

I figured that when we got back, we would be praised for making the best of a bad situation, would be welcomed with open arms, given good positions again.

We had to be directly responsible for hundreds of thousands of souls in the underworld at this point.

That was nothing to sneeze at.

"Why is the screaming so loud?" Aram asked, looking over toward me for confirmation.

They always looked to me. Which was fitting. I was the eldest. I'd been in charge since we all accidentally found ourselves on the human plane. I tended to know and remember more about our ways, our history.

I had no answers for him, though.

Hell was full of screaming, of course, but when Daemon and Bael had been pulled through one of the Hellmouths, we hadn't heard it.

"That's it," Lenore said, jumping backward, clinging to Ly as his wing moved out, wrapping around her protectively as the rest of us took another couple of steps back as bursts of flames danced out of the hole, hotter and redder than flames on Earth.

"Fuck," Drex growled, half hunching forward, pressing his hands to his ears as the screaming intensified. It was such a sound that it felt like it slipped under your skin, vibrated your bones.

There was a loud popping noise, then a body on the ground before the open hole it had burst out of snapped closed.

But the screaming?

The screaming didn't stop.

Because the screaming was coming from the form in front of all of us, curled deep into a ball, covering her naked body.

Naked, yes, but so covered in blood that you could hardly make out that fact right away.

"Oh," Lenore yelped, trying to rush forward, but getting dragged backward by Lycus. "Someone has to help her," she insisted.

"We don't even know what she is," Drex objected.

"She looks human," Lenore said, but then shook her head at herself.

Of course she did.

We all did.

"I don't care who she is, can someone shut her up?" Drex growled, taking another couple steps back.

The woman's body convulsed hard, making the bloody hair slip off her shoulder.

And that was when I saw it.

A tattoo.

A familiar tattoo.

"Fuck," I snapped, rushing forward, dropping down on my knees, trying to reach out to her, but not seeing a single inch of her that didn't seem to be covered in a laceration of some sort.

"What's going on?" Lenore asked to my side as I felt Drex, Minos, and Aram move in around me. "Do they know her?" she added.

"That's Red," Lycus told her.

I'd been around for a long time.

I thought I was incapable of most human emotions, that my emotional range was set the same as it had been in hell. Rage and frustration were my dominant feelings most of the time.

But as my hand landed on what I thought was a safe space on Red's shoulder, and she let out a shriek as she wrenched away, I felt something unfamiliar, something I'd read about in books, but had never experienced myself.

It was something that made my stomach churn, that made my heart shoot upward. It was something that made a tingling, helpless sensation grip my system.

Fear.

This was what the humans talked of when they spoke of fear.

"What happened to her?" Drex asked, trying to brush the hair out of her face, cringing when he found her familiar features were unrecognizable. She was a swollen bruise.

"I don't know," I said, pulling off my coat, trying to cover her with it. "But we have to get her out of here."

"We have to get her a doctor," Aram insisted as he carefully bent down, scooped her, and pulled her to his chest.

"She'll heal," I reminded him. Because that was what we did. We healed. And usually pretty quickly.

I was trying to convince myself that she was so damaged from her trip, that coming through the Earth's core like that had roughed her up. Even as my logical side tried to remind me that Bael and Daemon had come from hell relatively unscathed, that all of us had once.

"We're going to have to gag her," Drex said as we made our way back out of the depths of the canyon, getting closer toward the area the humans were allowed to frequent. And despite it being the middle of winter and humans having no real natural defense against the cold, the idiots still went out and camped and shit no matter the weather.

Drex was right.

We had to gag Red.

Because despite being out, despite likely starting to heal, the screams were as ear-splitting as ever no matter how far we walked.

"Here," Bael said, ripping off a piece of his shirt, shoving it in her mouth.

"Lenore, give her your cloak," I demanded, getting a raised brow from Ly.

"We need to cover her completely or the humans are going to call the police. We all know that Red can't end up in a human hospital."

"It's fine," Lenore insisted, pulling off the antiquated garment I'd told her at least a dozen times made her stand out in human society—and not in a good way. She insisted it was something that reminded her of her upbringing, that she didn't care if it made her stand out.

Eventually, we made our way back to the SUV we'd rented to take this trip, none of us wanting to be on our bikes in the freezing cold if we could help it.

"What?" Aram asked, still holding Red on his lap in the car.

"I don't understand. She's not healing," I said, watching one small cut I'd been keeping an eye on for the whole drive back to our rental house. It was hardly more than a scratch. It should have healed in moments. But we were an hour into our drive and it was still bleeding and open.

"If you don't know, that's not good, right?" Daemon asked from the row behind us, looking over my shoulder. "You're the resident brain and all that."

He wasn't wrong.

And I had no answers.

"Maybe they just need to get cleaned out," Aram suggested. "Can't Lenore do some of her magical first aid on her?"

The only problem was, when we got back to the house and put Red down for Lenore to fuss over, not only did nothing she knew how to do work, but Red fought her every inch of the way. With fingernails, with teeth, with her fists and feet. Even with several of us holding her down, we could barely keep her still.

"I don't know what else to do," Lenore said later that night, so covered in blood that it looked like she'd been in one of those horror movies the humans loved so much. "I'm no healer," she added. "I only ever handled minor injuries in my coven. I... I don't know how to help her."

But someone needed to.

No, we couldn't die.

We could suffer, though.

And, clearly, Red was hurting.

She still needed to be kept gagged in case anyone within earshot could overhear her. Even with something muffling the sound, her screams were unrelenting.

I gave Lenore a nod, dismissing her, as I moved into the bedroom where Red was on the bed, a blanket draped over her damaged body.

"You gotta get someone," Drex said, moving in beside me. "You know what happens when someone is hurting for too long."

I did.

Because I'd done it to people over and over in the past.

Pain could drive someone insane a lot more quickly and easily than most would realize.

Drex was right.

This could go bad—*worse*—fast if we didn't help heal her.

"Alright. You get some drugs to get in her," I suggested. "I will find a doctor that can do something."

"How are you going to do that?" Drex asked, following me out of the room. "We're not like humans. They are going to realize. And then there will be questions."

"You let me handle that," I suggested, grabbing a coat that wasn't drenched in blood, and making my way out toward the car.

I didn't have a great plan. Which was unusual for me. Planning was what I did best. But there had been no way to prepare for this.

All I knew was Red needed someone to heal her.

And that I had to get that for her.

The consequences of it could be dealt with later. In a very final sort of way.

I rummaged in the SUV's trunk to find the couple of supplies I needed, shit normal people never kept around, but we always made sure we kept a supply of.

You never knew when you were going to need some handcuffs.

Or a gag.

Or even a suitcase big enough to stuff a body inside.

We'd learned that all the hard way over the years. So we were never unprepared if we didn't need to be.

And I needed to be prepared for this.

You didn't just go and snatch a human being off the streets without the right supplies.

At least not anymore.

Not with their alarm systems and large populations of do-gooders who wanted to step in and save someone in need.

I had no plan on who to take.

I watched two men in scrubs walk out first. Together. And each of them much harder targets.

It was an ugly but unavoidable fact that human women were just easier targets. Smaller, lighter, usually not as strong.

Then, like she was the one I'd been waiting for all along, a lone woman moved out the doors of the hospital, her hand raised, toying with the ends of her almost white-blonde hair, her brows drawn together, her lips pursed.

Beautiful.

There wasn't really any other way to describe her. Short, slight, with a pretty face with a sharp jaw, high cheekbones, and a lightly cleft chin, she practically looked half-fae under the harsh overhead lights in the parking lot.

She was lost in her own thoughts as she made her way down the lines of cars, making her way toward me, in fact.

Like fate.

If I believed in that bullshit.

You'd likely think I should have felt bad about my intentions.

Planning on snatching an innocent woman right off the street, taking her back to the house, using her to heal Red, then disposing of her because we couldn't exactly leave witnesses around who knew who we were, that we not only existed, but were part of their world.

That could never stand.

When we eventually all got back to hell, it would be the end of us.

We might not be able to die, but we could be made to suffer for all of eternity for that kind of fuck-up.

I had no intentions of having that be my future.

I didn't feel bad.

I had to heal Red.

Even if that meant sacrificing this human.

Chapter Two

Jo

I really didn't like my hair.

It was a silly thing to be harping on so much, but in between tasks all day at work, it was what I defaulted back to.

See, I had done it.

The thing we all say—when we are of sound mind and strong of heart—we will never do again.

I'd been tiptoeing that not-so-healthy mental line for a while, and after I subjected myself to a movie about a woman who "found herself" after taking off to a foreign country and falling in love, I had taken my wine-tipsy self to the bathroom with a pair of somewhat sharp shears and the belief that a new hairstyle would somehow shake me out of the funk I'd been in for months now.

I'd loved it as I stood there right after, adrenaline—and let's not forget the aforementioned wine—still coursing through my system.

But after a halfway decent night of sleep, a shower, and some fresh eyes, I had different feelings. Namely, ones that almost made me late for work because I was frantically trying to find a way to wear it that I liked.

You didn't exactly have a lot of options when you took your once waist-length blonde hair and cut it into a long bob that just barely brushed your shoulders.

I'd once heard that shorter hair made you look older, but it somehow had an adverse reaction for me. I felt like I looked like a child. Which was not what I was going for during my first month at my new job where everyone was already struggling to get to know me and gauge my skills.

I had this particularly tough head nurse who, for some reason or another, decided on sight that she wasn't my biggest fan. All I could think of as I made my way to work that day was her giving me that now legendary side-eye that managed to make me feel very small for any little infraction.

She'd already shown massive displeasure in my tendency to hum a little bit to myself while filling out charts. She also thought I was a pen thief (I am not). And I'd heard her talking to one of the other nurses complaining that I'd brought a magazine with me to flip through during my break instead of socializing.

It took a lot of self-control not to turn the corner and inform her that if maybe she were more welcoming,

I would have happily spent my break talking to some of them.

As it was, I felt like an outsider.

So even changing my hair felt like it was bringing unnecessary attention to me that was getting me more hard looks whenever it was mentioned.

I was never so glad to be done with a shift as I gathered my things, wondering if I had enough time to stop off at the store to grab some hair accessories that might help me tame this much shorter hair into some sort of style, so it wasn't such a reminder of my stupid mistake as I let it grow back in.

That was what was on my mind as I walked out of the hospital.

There was a bite in the air that shook off the lingering exhaustion that started to cling to me on my third twelve-hour shift in a row. I liked to stack them when I could, giving me a longer span off in between. I always found I decompressed better when I had time and space for it. So a day off in the middle of long shifts usually left me feeling frazzled and irritable.

I had one more shift in me this week, though. Someone else had called out, and after moving to a new area, a whole new state, in fact, I felt like I couldn't turn down the money from an extra shift after I'd used most of my savings to cover the move.

But then I was free for a few days. I had grand plans in store, let me tell you. Like re-grouting my bathtub and painting my moldings. Maybe squeezing in a trip to Ikea for some cute, but budget-friendly, pieces of furniture to add to my very bare space.

You see, when you break up with someone in a blind rage and storm out of the house you shared for three years, you didn't think to tell him that you'd be back for the eight-hundred-dollar couch you bought or all the various knick-knacks that he never even noticed existed.

I don't know about you, but I had always had too much pride to go back after a full-on rage-out like that.

I'd used cuss words that would make my mother embarrassed to claim me as her own. If she were still alive. As it was, she was probably ranting and raving in the afterlife about how she raised me better.

And she had.

I was raised by a mother who put a full face of makeup on the morning after her husband let her know that he'd been diddling the secretary for a year and a half, she was pregnant, and he had to "do the right thing" by her. A mother who bit her lip to save her face. A mother who once cut the tip of her middle finger off while chopping vegetables for Thanksgiving dinner and let out a very tame "Oh, fudge!" that she then apologized for.

I didn't know where my potty mouth came from, but I knew what got it flapping with reckless abandon.

Shitty men.

Shitty men doing shitty things.

Especially when those shitty men did shitty things to good women.

Oh, sure, I was no saint, but I had my heart in the right place, I did my best, I pulled my weight, I abided by the laws—both criminal and common decency.

So I felt I was justified in cussing out the man who sat me down to inform me that he needed to "keep his options open" after three years of monogamy, that he had to know if there was more out there for him.

More out there for him.

More than *me* out there for him.

Now, I'd loved the man—or thought I had at the time—so I'd overlooked a great many things about him while we dated. Like the fact that he always waited until the server walked away, then passed the check to me before sliding it back to himself to hand to the server when he returned.

Or that he worked a very part-time job because he was "working on his side-hustle" that seemed to involve playing a hell of a lot of video games and no actual hustling.

I never mentioned his complete disregard for our home that he refused to ever help me clean.

I didn't lose my ever-loving mind when he brought clippers with him and *cut his nails in bed*, leaving little toenail shrapnel all around.

Did I freak out when Valentine's went by and he "forgot?" No.

Did I speak up when I'd spent months researching, tracking down, and purchasing the perfect present for his mother for her birthday only to have him claim it as his own?

Nope.

Didn't do that either.

But he thought he could do better than me?

Let's just say, I was very aware during my rant that followed his declaration that I hadn't truly been in love with him at all. Because there was no pain over losing him. Just anger. Just a bone-deep resentment. And a little bit of fear at the idea of being single again, starting over again, having no one in the whole world again.

That was why I moved states. I figured it would feel a little less sad to start over and be alone in a place that wasn't filled with memories of a time I spent with someone who never appreciated me.

If it weren't for my terrible hair choice and my stern superior, I would say things were going pretty well.

I had a place in a decent area.

I had a steady job with a good income.

I got to start decorating from scratch again.

And I was pretty sure I was finally ready to take the plunge and get myself a pet. Something that didn't mind being alone while I did long shifts. A cat or maybe even a set of bunnies so they could keep each other company while I was out.

Things were really starting to look up.

"Don't scream," the voice hissed in my ear as a hand clamped over my mouth, as another grabbed me around the center, lifting me up off my feet, leaving me peddling in the air as he dragged me backward.

I'd been to a self-defense class that taught me exactly how to get out of this situation. I'd practiced it a dozen times. Successfully. But in the heat of the moment, the movements flew out of my brain, leaving only panic in their wake.

Even if I remembered the moves, I think it would have been over too fast to implement any of them.

One moment, I was walking out of work with the silliest cares in the world.

The next, I was tossed in the backseat of a SUV with a man on top of me.

Whatever panic I felt before amplified. My heartbeat pounded so loud that I heard the thumping of it in my ears, felt it in my throat, temples, wrists.

This was not happening.

I did not work so hard to change my life for the better only to be pulled into a car and raped on my way out of work one night.

One of my arms shot out, managing a sideways closed fist to the man's jaw under his mask, barely getting a muffled grunt out of him before I saw the handcuffs appear out of nowhere, closing around my wrist.

It was only a matter of seconds before he got the other wrist too, closing the bracelets so tight that they bit into my skin.

"Are you going to make me gag you?" he asked.

If he wanted me to be silent, then hell yes.

But I wasn't going to tell him that.

I shook my head vehemently as he looked down with me with light eyes, likely blue, the only thing visible to me.

Cold.

God, they were such cold eyes.

He searched me for a moment before deciding I was trustworthy, removing his hand.

I wasted exactly no time.

I opened my mouth to scream even as my feet pulled out from under him, ramming him in his lower stomach as I pushed toward the door near my head, trying to reach for the handle with my cuffed hands, tasting freedom, knowing that if I could just get out of the vehicle, that I had a much better chance of getting safe.

"Fucking hell," the man growled, hand clamping on my mouth as his body came down fully on mine, crushing my chest to the seat, his weight pinning me in place.

I was small.

Short, petite, "doll-like" my mother used to say.

I stood no chance against a man who had to be well over six feet with the weight that came with such a tall frame.

"This will be easier for you if you stop fighting it," he growled in my ear as his hand slipped away, but only because he planted it at the back of my head, smashing my face into the material seats that smelled like, oh God, like blood.

But before I could truly slip into the horror of that realization, something was slipping over my mouth, getting tied so tight around the back of my head that I immediately started to get a headache.

"Alright, down you go," he declared. And before I could guess his meaning, he was pushing me off the seat and onto the floor, wrestling with my cuffed wrists and another set of handcuffs until he attached me to a bar under the seat.

And with that, he climbed out of the back like nothing at all had happened, getting into the front, turning over the car, and backing out of the spot.

All the while, in my mind, all I heard was the animated voice of the true crime podcaster I loved listening to talking in my head.

Don't ever let them take you to a second location.

We all knew what happened at second locations.

But, as the car pulled out of my work lot, and the bar under the seat refused to budge no matter how hard I yanked against it, it didn't seem like I had any say in the matter.

All I could do now was try to stop letting the panic fog my brain. I needed to think. I needed to focus. Because wherever he was taking me next, he would have to get into the backseat again and unfasten me from the bar.

If I kept my wits about me, if I looked for the right opening, I might be able to act quickly enough to get away, to flag down a passing car, run to a neighbor's house.

Something.

Anything.

So he drove.

I plotted.

When the car pulled to a stop, anticipation skittered across my nerve endings, made me feel jumpy and strangely weightless.

The door opened at my feet, and the car jolted a bit as the man climbed inside, and unfastened the second set of cuffs from the bar.

Alright.

So I didn't give it a whole ton of thought, as it turned out.

I just reacted in the moment in the best way I could. Which meant I struck outward with the swinging cuffs, knocking the man across the bridge of his nose. It didn't have the kind of impact I wanted what with the face mask on to soften the blow and all.

But it gave me a second of shocked inaction that allowed me to scramble toward the other door, wrenching it open, and tossing myself out the other side.

I wasn't even sure I was seeing right as I took off. My vision was so blinded by my fear that I ran in the exact opposite direction we had come from. You know, the direction that had led to a road at some point. A road where I might encounter cars and people who could help me.

Nope.

I made a beeline for what was a whole lot of nothing. Except an open field that led up to a mountain that made my thigh muscles burn just looking at it.

But I couldn't seem to find any logical thoughts right then. Like the ones that would tell me to turn around, change directions, head back to the road.

I was in pure fight-or-flight response right about then. And all I could think about was running, getting away, not letting him drag me wherever he was planning to, do whatever he wanted to me while I was helpless but to endure it.

I didn't even hear him approaching.

But I felt his fingers sinking into my upper arm, the strength in them hurting, bruising.

I didn't think of anything but yanking away.

Because had I thought about it, I might have realized that the momentum would have sent me shooting forward, that I couldn't brace myself properly thanks to the cuffs, that I would be helpless to do anything but fall

And crack my head off the ground.

And slip into the inky blackness of unconsciousness.

So, yeah, that was exactly what I did.

Chapter Three

Ace

"Did you kill her?" Drex asked, coming up behind me as I leaned over the woman whose body was very still on the ground.

"She fell," I told him, reaching out to flip her onto her back, brushing her hair out of her face to look at the bloody wound on her head.

"You realize she's not going to be able to help Red if she's bleeding in her brain, right?" he asked, sounding amused as he rocked back on his heels.

"You're not helping."

"I'm not known for it," he agreed.

"Make yourself useful then, and get Lenore. She might not be able to help Red, but she can probably do something about this," I said, waving at the woman's head.

Hearing Drex move off—even if it was at a snail's pace—I looked back at the woman, turning her head each way to make sure she hadn't hurt herself anywhere else before letting my gaze slip down, seeing a laminated hospital badge hanging from a clip low by her hip.

Curious, I grabbed it, finding her name there.

Josephine Walsh.

RN.

I'd been hoping for a doctor. But I figured the nurses did a lot of the work at any given hospital. They certainly did most of the wound care. She should have been able to handle whatever was going on with Red.

"Oh, no," Lenore said, rushing forward, taking in the handcuffs, the wound on the woman's face. "What did you do?" she accused, dropping down, fingers pressing around the cut.

"Got someone to heal Red."

"And who is going to heal her?" Lenore asked, frustration clear in her voice.

It was no secret that she'd never been a fan of mine. Over her time with us, she'd developed relationships with most of the others, maybe especially so Daemon and Aram, the least cold of all of us. But she'd also gotten close with Minos. I'd walked down to get coffee many-a-morning to find the two of them talking in hushed whispers in the kitchen. She also often asked Seven for help with some task or another. She tolerated Drex and his sarcastic indifference. And she kept a wide berth around Bael. Like all of us did, to be honest. The man was not someone who wanted to get to know anyone, form any sort of relationships.

But me?

She openly disliked me much of the time.

I rarely gave her reason to feel otherwise.

"You," I told her, reaching down to lift the nurse off the ground. "It doesn't look that bad."

Lenore followed me inside, mumbling under her breath the whole time as I brought the woman into my bedroom where Red was still on the bed, bleeding, screaming against her gag.

"Fix up her head. Stay with her. Then call me when she wakes up," I demanded to Lenore as I placed the nurse on the couch, then made my way toward the door, needing coffee, to sit in front of the fire, to get some warmth back in my body after being outside for so long.

"Barking orders at her," Ly said as I moved into the kitchen, shaking his head at me. "Easy with that shit. You're my boss, not hers."

"If she didn't talk shit to me all the time, I wouldn't need to bark at her," I shot back as I went to the coffee maker, brewing a pot.

We didn't get a boost from caffeine like humans did, and I found myself envious of their susceptibility to mind and body altering chemicals as the day started to weigh on me. It was early to feel tired, but as I cradled my coffee in my hands and moved in front of the fire Bael was stoking, I knew that this tired wasn't as simple as needing rest.

I was a different kind of tired.

Just life tired.

Exhausted, really.

After finding out Lenore was capable of what generations of witches never could manage—opening the mouths of hell for us—I'd started to let myself hope for something I'd scarcely let myself truly hope for before.

A return home.

It had always been my goal, one I worked doggedly toward, one I obsessed about, but a part of me had always been doubtful it would be possible. Or, at least, that it would be possible for several generations yet.

I always figured that, worst case, eventually there would be a war between Good and Evil. And if Lucifer himself decided to open up a Hellmouth, we would have a way to go home.

But then there was Lenore with her powers, with her control over them.

She'd opened the Hellmouth that had produced Bael and Daemon, the same Hellmouth that Red had jumped into in her excitement over getting home after so long.

There had been a restless excitement among all of us since then. Even after several failures. We all figured it was just a matter of time before we found the right Hellmouth with enough energy left to open it.

I'd been sure as the Earth started dropping down into its own core that this was it, all the years on this plane were finally over, and I could take most of my men back home.

Not having that happen, then having Red show up so mutilated, it was more than my body wanted to deal with, let alone my mind.

I needed a few minutes to sort it out in my head before I could go back there.

"What?" I asked, sensing Bael's gaze on me.

"She didn't get fucked up like that just coming through," he told me, making me turn, finding his eyes intense, his jaw tight.

"I'd deduced that already," I agreed.

"So it stands to reason that someone did that."

He wasn't wrong.

"I've seen wounds like that on her back before," he said. "I've inflicted wounds like that before," he went on. "As I'm sure you have." I didn't want to think about it. I didn't want to come to conclusions about it. "Someone lashed her," he finished.

Yes.

There was no way around that fact.

Those lacerations were ones I'd seen a million times in my very long life. Both in hell and on the human plane.

If humans ever believed they were fundamentally good, all you had to do was go back in history a little bit to see how evil many of them were. Lashings and beheadings and burning at the stake. Even those who didn't inflict the pain stood by and witnessed it, took part in it, found glee in it.

"Yes," I agreed, turning back to the fire.

The questions were... who... and why?

Red could be a lot to handle if you weren't used to her. She could be cocky and forward. She liked to push buttons.

Time moves differently down there. For us, it had been a year and a half, give or take. For her, it had been decades. Long enough to possibly make some enemies, push someone's buttons.

We didn't usually attack one another. That was the base, animalistic shit that the humans did. We punished the humans. That was where we took our rage out.

At least, that was how it used to be, how it had always been.

But who knew what had changed since then.

"Was this commonplace?" I asked, hating having to defer to Bael, but recognizing that I was not the expert in this one way.

"Lashing each other?" he clarified. "No."

"Did it ever happen?"

"Not that I ever saw."

"Hopefully once she is healed, she will be in her right mind again. Then she can tell us what happened," I said, shrugging.

I was a facts-based man. It seemed a waste of time to speculate, bat around ideas that may or may not be true. It was better to wait, to get the information right from the source.

One glance into my bedroom showed Lenore fussing over the nurse's head, muttering under her breath. Whether it was words of encouragement or actual spells, I had no idea. I didn't give a shit. So long as she got her up and working on Red.

"What?" I asked when Drex jerked his chin toward the front room.

"Aram," he said, swirling his glass before taking a sip.

Sighing, I gave up my plans of grabbing a book and getting lost for a while before the nurse woke up and could give us some answers.

"Aram," I called, walking into the front room to find him sitting off the edge of the couch, his head buried in his hands.

"She didn't deserve this."

"No one is saying she did," I said.

"No one is worried about her. You just tossed her on a bed with a gag in her mouth."

"Because I needed to go get someone to help her. I did that. I did what I could do. I think we can all agree that hand-holding and comforting is not my department."

It was more of his, though.

And judging by the blood all over him, he had tried.

Unsuccessfully, it seemed, by his defeated posture.

"She shrieked when I tried to touch her hand."

"She's in pain, Aram," I reminded him.

It was easy to forget pain since we so seldom felt it, and when we did, it was fleeting. And Aram had led a much more charmed life on Earth than I had.

It may have been hundreds of years before, but I still vividly remembered how it felt to have a knife stuck in my stomach and yanked upward, slicing through everything within.

I'd been shot a few times since then, but nothing compared to being gutted like that. The pain had lasted for hours before I finally healed.

I imagined Red felt like that, but from head-to-toe.

"Why isn't she healing?" he asked, needing answers, ones I didn't have for him.

"I don't know," I admitted.

Which was why I wanted to go read. True, the humans didn't have the most comprehensive information about our kind, but some of the old texts had some insights in them that might prove useful.

It wasn't like I carried around ancient texts with me. Hell, it wasn't like I even owned many myself. But the humans had come a long way the past hundred or so years. I had an endless number of scanned ancient texts on my tablet that I could access at any time.

Which was how I planned to spend the rest of my evening if the nurse didn't wake up.

Trying to get answers.

So I could pass them onto my men.

So they didn't keep looking at me like I'd let them down.

I'd avoided that for generations by being proactive, by always being the first to know things, to learn things, so they never had to feel lost in this world as it changed around us.

It was the least I could do.

As the leader.

I'd never felt as undeserving of that title as I did when we all watched Red scream and refuse to heal, and have no explanations for them.

"I will figure it out," I assured Aram. "Why don't you go reach out to the local bikers and see if you can score some better pain medicine. Seems like whatever we gave her isn't cutting it."

"Yeah, okay," he agreed, hopping up, eager for a mission, some way to not feel so useless.

"Take Seven with you. He has a friend who is a patched member."

And it was two of them out of my hair while we tried to figure shit out.

With that, I took off to Aram's room to get some quiet so I could read in peace.

It was several hours later that I heard her.

Not Lenore telling me the nurse was awake.

Oh, no.

The nurse herself, yelling.

I guess I was up.

With a sigh, I put down my tablet, and made my way toward my room to deal with her.

Chapter Four

Jo

The screaming inside my skull was the first thing I became aware of as unconsciousness slowly pulled backward like a fog in the early morning light.

I'd suffered from migraines in the past, and this pain was like that, but amplified, making me try to raise my hands to press the heels to my forehead, always finding that the pressure helped with the pain.

But when I tried to lift them, I felt resistance. As soon as I became aware of that, the pain around my wrists vied for acknowledgment.

It was right then that it all rushed back.

Leaving work.

Worrying about my hair.

Hands.

A body.

A man.

A car.

Cuffs.

A gag.

Trying to break free, tripping, and then nothing.

That nothing was because I'd probably hit my head. Which explained the jackhammering sensation in my temple.

My eyes flew open as I tried to scramble up to a seated position, finding my vision refused to focus for a long second as my stomach flipped, making bile rise up in my throat.

Possible concussion.

That wasn't the least bit surprising, what with not having been able to properly brace my fall and everything.

Squeezing my eyes shut, I took a couple deep breaths, trying to fight back the dizziness and nausea.

The gag was gone, I realized, but felt the remnants of its existence in an aching across my lips, cheeks, and around the back of my head.

"You're okay," a soft female voice declared at my side, making me jolt as my eyes shot open.

Then there she was.

A beautiful woman with long dark black hair that made me miss mine for one absurdly inappropriate second. She was dressed strangely too, in some sort of floor-sweeping green gown with long sleeves. It was a dress out of time, something meant for period piece movies, not modern times, sitting right in front of me on a footstool.

I thought it was a trick of light at first but as she shifted, the lamp shined on her face, making her small tattoo stand out against her pale skin. It was a light blue crescent moon at her uppermost point of her forehead, the pointed edges disappearing up into her hairline.

I'd seen plenty of tattoos in my day, everything from a Miss Piggy pin-up holding a riding crop to the bare ass of Kermit the Frog to an actual Nazi swastika, and everything in between.

I'd never seen one quite like hers before, though.

"Where am I?" I asked, tension uncurling in my stomach.

"Ah, what did they say? Utah, I think," she said, seeming confused by the word.

Of course we were in Utah.

"What is this place?" I asked, eyes begging her to understand.

"Oh, a house. A rental house," she added, giving me an encouraging smile. "You had a bad fall. You cut your forehead," she told me. "I cleaned it out and packed it with a poultice."

A poultice?

Who even used that word anymore, let alone knew how to mix one together?

The part of me that had spent a lot of time learning proper wound care by our modern standards was having a mild heart attack at the idea of some hippie woman playing herbalist putting God-knew what herbs or leaves or spit in my open wound.

But there would be time to worry about that later.

After I got myself free, got away, got some help.

Maybe this woman could help.

But it was right about then that a strange noise sounded from behind me. A muted, shrieking sound, something that immediately put me on edge as I turned, looked back, and found a large bed behind me.

With a mostly naked woman on top.

Completely covered in blood.

With a gag in her mouth.

There was a knee-jerk, selfish moment where I worried about that being me, that I was maybe taken to replace her when he was done with her very badly abused body.

The thoughts were replaced almost instantly, though, with concern. For her. For her wellbeing. For her obvious pain as she screamed against her gag.

"What happened to her?"

"I, ah, I can't tell you that," the woman said, shaking her head.

"What do you mean you can't tell me? Who did that to her? Who are you protecting?" I demanded, voice rising.

Let's just say that I had seen far too many women come into the hospitals I'd worked at with clear signs of abuse from men who'd driven them in for care. And despite trying my best, sometimes, I could never get through to the women, could never get them help.

And it made me have a hair trigger when it came to abusers. And those who enabled them through inaction.

"Lower your voice," another voice joined the conversation. Lower, deeper. Masculine. "Or I will have to put the gag back on you," he added as my gaze lifted, finding a man standing in the doorway, swallowing up the whole space.

He'd had a mask on, of course, but his size was familiar. Tall, strong but not overly bulky. I felt reasonably confident saying this was the man who had abducted me, who had wrestled me into his car, who had cuffed and gagged me, who had chased me until I fell.

Then, apparently, dragged me inside and sicced his brainwashed female friend on me.

"How about no?" I shot back, jaw tight.

I should have been scared. But I found a surprising amount of anger coursing through my system, making my skin feel electric, my jaw tight.

"What are you going to do? Hit me again?" I added.

"You hit your own fucking head," he reminded me, looking infuriatingly amused by that fact.

I didn't want to think it, but it was impossible not to notice, even in this situation.

The man was gorgeous.

Like Adonis, Greek sculpture, belongs in an art gallery or fancy cologne ad kind of gorgeous.

It was the perfect, classical bone structure with a chiseled jaw, a Greek nose, a high, proud forehead, and stern brows over ice blue eyes that almost seemed to have flecks of a different color in them, but he was too far away to make them out.

His hair was blond and perfectly styled even after having worn a ski mask to kidnap me.

He was dressed like he was planning on spending time outdoors with a tan grandpa sweater over a hooded sweatshirt.

It was hot in the house. Like uncomfortably so. How he wasn't sweating like crazy was beyond me.

"Maybe I wouldn't have hit my head if I wasn't trying to escape a violent psychopath kidnapper," I said, shooting him my best mean face.

He completely ignored me, looking over at the other woman instead. "Lenore, go on. Ly has been waiting impatiently in your room," he said as the woman gave me one last long look before moving away.

"Let me go," I demanded, trying for strong, but with the absence of the woman, I was feeling a lot less comfortable.

Why would he send her away?

So he could do terrible things to me without an audience?

"No," he said, moving over toward the bed, looking down at the woman there.

"What did you do to her?" I demanded, anger rising again as she writhed in pain.

"Nothing."

"Oh, so she hit herself all over and cut herself all over too?" I asked. "How coincidental that things like that keep happening around you, huh?"

"You're not here to run your mouth," he informed me in that cool tone of his.

"Why am I here then?" I asked, trying to wriggle my wrists around, get them loose, but he had the cuffs on me too tight.

"To heal her," he said, wincing a bit as the woman on the bed shrieked against her gag when he tried to brush her bloody hair out of her face.

"Why wouldn't you bring her to the hospital?" I asked.

"For reasons that are none of your fucking business. Just get over here and look her over. Tell me what you need to fix her, and I will have someone get it."

Not sure I had a choice, I rose from the couch, feeling my vision swim for a moment before it settled and I could continue across the room, going to the opposite side of the bed than him.

The woman was completely covered in blood.

And it was no wonder.

Because her back looked like it had been whipped, the lacerations deep and long, criss-crossing her entire back from shoulders down to lower hips. There was even one deep lash mark across her butt.

"How long ago did she get these?" I asked, somehow able to think past my kidnapping and focus on the task at hand. But as I raised my hands to try to push her hair out of the way, the cuffs were a painful reminder of my situation.

I raised them at him, giving him a hard look.

To that, he searched my face for a long moment before moving around the bed, coming around to tower over me, reaching out with one hand to encircle my wrist to see the lock, then pulling out the key.

There was not—was absolutely not—a strange little electrical current that coursed over my skin when his fingertips brushed me. Because that would make no sense whatsoever.

"Don't even think about running," he told me, voice low, lethal, drawing my head up to look at his face. "I have men everywhere," he added, holding my gaze for a long second, making me realize that those specks I'd seen in his light blue eyes were actually, well, red. Except that made no sense. Because people didn't have red accents in their eyes.

"I'm not going to promise to be a good little captive," I told him, watching as his lips twitched ever so slightly before they fell back into their stern line.

"Fix Red," he demanded, pulling the cuffs off fully, then moving toward the other side of the room, leaning back against the wall near the door.

I tried not to notice, but there was no way to avoid feeling his gaze on me as I reached out toward the woman—Red—moving her hair, so I could see the outer edges of the wounds better.

They weren't puffy and red like they were older, like they had time to get infected. They seemed fresh.

"These all need to be stitched," I told him, checking out each individual slice for any tiny sign of infection that would need to be left open to drain.

"Give me a list of items," he demanded, curt, no-nonsense.

"A suture kit. Gauze. Saline solution. Antibiotic cream. Some actual antibiotics. Oral. She needs to be in a hospital," I insisted, looking over at him, shaking my head. "This is bad. She needs medical attention."

"She has it. That's why you're here."

"This isn't a sterile environment. I don't have—"

"I told you to give me a fucking list," he interrupted me. "Whatever it is, I can get it," he told me, not a hint of uncertainty in his words. And I guess if you were willing to kidnap a nurse to treat someone, stealing medical supplies wasn't a big deal.

"Everything I just mentioned," I said, feeling it was useless to argue. If she wasn't going to go to the hospital, then I had to treat her to the best of my ability. "Pain medicine. She's screaming. You don't hear her screaming?" I asked, voice tense.

"I have someone getting her pain medicine," he told me, shrugging. "What else?"

Ignoring him, I moved around the bed, inspecting some minor cuts and bruises under the blood on the woman's thighs, legs. They were worse on the bottom of her feet.

"Oh, God," I hissed, feeling my stomach flip over, making me need to take a steadying breath.

"What?" the man asked, not sounding any more concerned than he'd been a moment before.

"Someone removed... did you do this?" I asked, whipping around, ignoring the swirling of my vision, shooting daggers at him.

"Did I do *what*?" he asked, voice just as cutting as mine.

"Remove all her toenails," I clarified, even thinking of it making me feel sick again. I had a tough stomach when it came to all the various injuries a body could have inflicted upon it.

Two things freaked me out.

Toenails broken off.

And piercings being ripped out.

It was probably because they reminded me of horror movies I'd seen at way too young an age, ones that had stuck with me no matter how hard I tried to shake them.

"What?" he asked, pushing off the wall, taking long-legged strides across the room, moving to stand shoulder-to-shoulder with me, bending forward to inspect her feet.

I felt a wave of relief when I realized he hadn't done this. He wouldn't need to inspect his handiwork if he had.

So maybe I wasn't going to end up on a bed covered in my own blood after all.

When the man straightened, I didn't see the shock or horror or disgust I felt myself, just a blankness, a resolve even.

"Do you need anything specific for that?"

"Uhm, not right now. When they heal—if they heal—she might want some glue."

"Glue?"

"To put on the nail beds," I told him. "Your nail beds are sensitive. They feel sore if they are exposed. The glue would protect them and stop the soreness."

"Got it. Anything else?" he asked, not bothering to move out of my way, making me squeeze in front of him to move to the other side of the bed, my whole back brushing against his front.

I tried to inspect the woman's front without pushing her onto her back. "Ice packs," I decided, seeing how swollen her face was, her eyes nothing but little slits above dark black eyes. "Maybe some braces or elastic bandages?" I said, shrugging. "I don't know if anything is broken," I clarified. "I don't want to touch her without cleaning her wounds first. Oh, and gloves. I'll need gloves."

"Alright. I will get all of that," he agreed, turning, making his way back toward the door, closing it with a loud snap, making me jump.

"I don't know if you are in your right mind right now," I said to the woman, feeling a sting of tears at the backs of my eyes as she screamed against her gag. "But I am going to try everything I can to get you out of pain and well again. Whoever did this to you is a monster," I added, sitting down on the very edge of the bed, at a loss for what to do until I had the supplies I needed, so starting to hum because it was the only comfort I could give her.

The door opened a couple of minutes later, making my heart leap up as I looked over my shoulder.

But it wasn't the man from before.

This one was tall as well, but a little rougher-around-the-edges looking with his dark hair, beard, jeans, boots, and a leather vest thing over a black t-shirt.

"Sorry, babe," he said, making his way toward the windows, and it was right then that I noticed the hammer and box of nails in his hand. "Ace said I gotta seal off your exits," he told me.

Ace.

The other man's name was Ace.

"Did you do this to her?" I asked him as he grabbed a nail, held it against the frame of the window.

"Fuck no."

That was it.

Fuck no.

But at least I knew that was two of the people in this house who wouldn't pull out my toenails. It was a small sort of comfort, but I was going to take all that I could get.

The sound of the hammer seemed to ricochet through my skull, making my body jolt with each strike, leaving me feeling jumpy even after he was done.

"Uhm, excuse me, Mr..."

"Drex," he corrected, looking horrified at me calling him mister. "Just Drex."

"Drex," I repeated, finding the name clumsy on my tongue. "Can I have some water?"

To that, he shrugged.

"Guess I can manage that," he agreed, moving off, closing the door behind him.

Maybe I should have been trying to see if I could grab the heads of the nails and rip them out of the window, get myself out of there.

But if I left, this woman was probably going to die. And I wasn't sure I was heartless enough to let that happen. Maybe I'd never taken the Hippocratic Oath, but I'd never been the kind of person who could watch someone hurting and not at least try to help.

I would get her cleaned up and stitched up as best as I could, then I would try to find a way out of this situation.

Because they weren't just going to let me go, right?

I mean, I'd seen their faces.

Sure, as a couple hours passed, the Lenore woman and Drex's faces started to blur in my memory. For some reason, though, Ace's face was tattooed on my mind.

But only because I'd seen him for longer, of course. That was the only rational explanation.

If they let me go, I could absolutely give a police sketch artist enough to go on for Ace.

"Here," Drex said, coming back with a wine glass full of water.

"Thank you," I said, trying to give him a smile even though it felt—and likely looked—fake. "That other guy was a, ah—"

"Dick?" Drex asked, smirking. "Go on, you can say it."

"Well, yeah," I agreed.

"Don't get it twisted, blondie," he said, shaking his head. "We're all motherfuckers here. Save the smiles for someone else. You aren't going to butter me up."

With that, he was gone again, leaving me feeling very foolish for thinking there was something good inside these men to appeal to. Good men brought horrifically injured women to the hospital. Even if all they did was drop them off at the emergency room and ran off out of fear of getting implicated.

Alone as the time dragged on, I found myself pacing the room, humming at first to try to comfort the woman. Then, as minutes turned to hours, to soothe myself.

"Here's your shit," Ace said, making me jump, a stifled scream escaping me as I turned, finding him already moving into the room when I hadn't even heard him open the door.

I decided not to concern myself with his bloody hands.

It wasn't my business how he got the supplies.

And whatever he had done to get them wasn't my fault just because I needed them.

At least that was what I was trying to convince myself of as I laid everything out on the dresser, rearranging it in the order I thought I would need.

"Ace, here," yet another voice said, making me turn to find two more men moving into the room.

Both were tall.

One was dark-skinned with loc'd hair and a more muscular, stockier build.

The other was a little thinner with inky black hair kept a little long and tanned skin that maybe spoke of Middle Eastern descent.

Both had brown eyes.

And both appeared to have those strange red flecks in theirs as well.

What the hell was that about?

"What is that?" I asked as the Black man handed Ace a bottle.

"Goodfellas," the other man supplied, looking me over.

Goodfellas.

You didn't work in hospital rooms without learning a few street names for drugs.

Goodfellas. China Girl. Dance fever. He-man.

They'd gotten fentanyl.

Which was fifty to a hundred times more potent than morphine.

"Ace told us to get something strong," the Middle Eastern looking man supplied. "Is that strong enough?"

"They use it after surgery," I supplied. "So, yes."

"Will it be enough to knock her out while you work on her?" he pressed.

God, I hoped so.

I couldn't imagine doing what I needed to do to the woman if she was conscious.

"But, um, I still might need all of you to help hold her down," I told them, even if the idea of all three of them in the room put me on-edge.

"Whatever Red needs," he agreed, sounding pained. "She's a good friend," he supplied, to what must have been a question in my eyes.

"Aram," Ace called to the man who was speaking to me. "Go get some water. You are going to need water, right?" he asked, looking at me.

"Yes. Right," I agreed, taking a steadying breath as I moved toward the woman. "I need to take the gag off to get the medicine in," I told them.

Ace brushed past me, none too ceremoniously ripping the gag off the woman. Who immediately started screaming at the top of her lungs—a raw, animalistic sound that made a chill wash over me, leaving me paralyzed as the sounds she made seemed to wipe all thoughts out of my head.

"The fuck are you doing?" Ace yelled. "Get your ass over here and give her the medicine."

Snapping out of it, I rushed forward, shaking a pill into my hand, then pressing it down the woman's throat, feeling like something was lodged in mine as I did so.

"What the hell was that?" he asked as he put the gag back in her mouth, shooting accusing eyes at me. "Is this your first week as a nurse? You've never heard someone in pain before?"

I had.

Of course, I had.

It was rare, though, that someone actually hit a ten on the pain scale. A ten was an unimaginable amount of pain, the kind that made you bedridden and delirious. Only a handful of people ever have to experience a ten.

This woman?

I'd swear this woman was experiencing a fifteen.

I'd never heard anything like it before.

Dread flooded my system at the idea of needing to cause her any more pain, even if it was going to help her in the long run.

"I think you got a stupid one," the other man in the room said, looking at me as I stood there, unable to remember what Ace had even said to me, let alone know how to appropriately answer.

"If you don't have anything helpful to say, Seven, shut the fuck up," Ace demanded, gaze slipping to me. "I think she might have jiggled her brain around in her skull when she fell," he supplied, looking at my forehead.

I'd forgotten all about the cut, about the poultice that was probably giving me a raging infection as each moment passed.

"Concussion," I supplied.

"What?"

"When your brain hits your skull. It's called a concussion."

"See? Not stupid," Ace said, giving Seven a stern look. "You gonna start this shit or what?" he asked, looking back at me.

I wanted to wait until the pain medicine kicked in. But there wasn't much time to waste.

I had to get to work.

Chapter Five

Ace

She was impressive once she got out of her head and onto the task at hand.

I'd seen all sorts of healers in the human realm. From women in their huts in the woods, doling out garlic and honey salves for infections to battlefield doctors giving men bullets to bite down on while they hacked away at their infected limbs with old, filthy saws. I hadn't witnessed a lot of modern medicine up close, though.

The nurse's moves were practiced and precise. No shaking hands. No second-guessing what she was meant to do. There was a set order of things and she went through it until, a few hours later, she climbed back off the bed, scrubs, arms, and gloved hands covered in blood and sweat.

"Okay. That's it," she said, taking a deep breath, letting it out shakily. "You have antibiotics?" she asked, looking over at me.

Aram and Seven had made their way out when Red stopped fighting the ministrations, likely heading to their beds as the sun started to streak in through the windows.

"Yes," I said, moving over toward the bag I'd brought in, finding the three separate bottles, and bringing them over to her. "I had no idea which was strongest."

"This one," she said, taking the bottle. "Does she have any allergies?"

"Not that I've seen," I told her, shrugging, finding my mind sluggish with lack of rest and the stress that had slipped in under my skin and set up house.

"Okay," she said, going over toward Red, removing the gag, and shoving the pill down her throat. "She's quieter," she said, going to reach out toward her face, but seeming to remember at the last second that when anyone put a hand on Red, she started screaming and fighting again. "Can we leave the gag off?" she asked, looking over at me. "I will be able to hear her if something is wrong then," she added.

"Yeah, fine," I agreed, nodding.

"Would it be possible if I could, um, you know," she said, waving a hand down at her bloodstained body.

"Yeah," I agreed, sighing, leading her toward the door and out into the hall. "Through here," I said, opening the door to the bathroom. "No," I snapped when she moved in then reached up to close the door. "The door stays open."

"I need to shower," she insisted, those brown eyes of hers going round.

"Yeah, tough shit," I said. "Shower with the door open, or don't shower at all."

Her teeth gritted at that.

There was no fucking logical reason not to let her close the door. The bathroom didn't even have a window, just a fan in the ceiling to let the hot air out.

"You can't be serious," she insisted, eyes starting to get glassy. I hadn't seen a woman cry in fucking ages. I found it oddly fascinating, even if I knew that wasn't the appropriate reaction. By human standards.

"Yet somehow I am. I can take you back to the room like that if you want."

Her lower lip trembled at that as the first tear slipped down her cheek.

I had the most uncharacteristic, asinine urge to move closer and catch that tear with my finger.

"P...please," she said, head lowering, gaze moving to the floor.

"Halfway," I agreed. I was not, ever, known as someone who compromised, who changed his mind.

Yet one little plea from a complete stranger, and I was going back on my word.

I just needed rest.

I was running on empty.

That was the only explanation.

"Thank you," she said, but refused to look at me as she turned and made her way toward the garbage, shucking off her gloves, then reaching inside the glass shower stall to turn on the water.

I watched for a minute longer than I had a right to as she pulled her scrub top upward to discard it on the floor, showing me a gently sloped back with a deep red bra band and what looked like some sort of tattoo at the back of her neck.

But I managed to shake myself out of it, closing the door halfway like I'd told her I would, then making my way back toward my room, going into the dresser to grab one of my long-sleeve tees. It was pointless to get her any pants. Anything I had would fall right off of her.

I would ask Lenore for something in the morning, but I was too tired to wake anyone else up and start demanding shit right then. She could make do with the shirt that would be more like a dress on her small frame.

With that, I grabbed a towel from the hall closet, and went into the bathroom.

I caught one glorious second of her completely bare self from her perky breasts with dusty pink nipples to the slope of her stomach, the gentle flare of her hips, her shapely if not overly long legs, and even the space between that made my cock stir in my pants, despite my pure exhaustion. But a shriek escaped her as her arms shot down, one draping across her breasts, the other covering the juncture of her thighs.

"Relax. Nothing I haven't seen a million times," I told her, going for dry and unimpressed, but finding my words came out tight, a little airless.

"Don't," she demanded, voice quivering.

"Don't what?" I asked, brows furrowing as I watched the water cascade over her shoulder, pooling where her arm was holding her breasts.

"Don't rape me," she demanded, voice choked.

"I don't fucking rape women," I snapped, more offended than I likely had a right to be. I had been eye-fucking her naked body after barging in on her shower.

I'd been around the humans for long enough to know that wasn't acceptable behavior.

Their customs changed a lot over the years, but a woman's modesty usually was something considered sacred, even if some human men always refused to respect it. We had a fun way to make rapists suffer back home. It involved a very slim hot poker that would be driven ever so slowly up their dick holes.

It was a fitting punishment for what they'd done. And the *screams*.

Fuck.

Those screams were music to our ears.

"Then why are you in here?" she asked, voice sharp.

"Towel," I said, showing it to her before hanging it on the hook. "Shirt," I told her, waving it before putting it on the sink counter. "You have five more minutes," I added, moving back into the hall, leaning back against the wall, feeling the pressure of my hard cock against my pants, trying to deep-breathe past it.

I wasn't a man controlled by his sex drive.

Did I fuck the women who came to our parties, who showed up at rallies? Sure I did. When someone was throwing pussy at you, it was stupid to turn it down.

But I didn't crave it when they weren't around.

The human concept of blue balls had always meant very little to me.

I was starting to have a personal understanding of what they were talking about.

The water cut off, and I had to actively force my thoughts to other things than her pert tits, her smooth skin, the soft, feminine folds of her pussy.

My hard-on was still raging when the door opened all the way, and there she was in my tee that swallowed up her body like I'd thought it would.

"Do you have a blanket?" she asked as I led her back to my room, motioning toward the couch.

"No. Go to sleep," I demanded, walking out of the room, closing the door, and moving into the living room.

I thought I would pass out as soon as my ass hit the cushion of the sofa. But I found my mind racing, ping-ponging between possibilities until I eventually felt wide awake, revved up even.

So I made coffee, feeling the heat chase away the chill of this world, the kind of cold that got amplified when you went without sleep. I tried to read, but found the words swimming on the page.

Finally, more worried about Red than I cared to admit to the others, knowing I needed to put on a calm and collected face for them, I snuck back into my bedroom, making my way toward the bed where she was writhing a bit again, though seemingly while asleep this time.

"You need to shake this shit off, Red," I demanded, sitting off the edge of the bed. "I need answers. The crew needs you back. Aram looks like a lost puppy," I added, sighing out my breath. "You should be healed by now. I don't understand what's happening. Shake this shit off, Red. You come back, and I will skin whoever did this to you."

We'd all hurt at the hands of humans in the past. Rival MCs got territorial or someone fucked the wrong guy's old lady or whatever stupid shit humans worried about. And it led to some sort of altercation. One where we needed to pretend to be weaker than we were, so no one caught on. Which meant we took a lot of blows.

But I had a sneaking suspicion that whatever was going on with Red had nothing to do with humans.

Even though I'd never heard of our own kind attacking one another.

If that was what happened though, I didn't care if it took another couple of generations, I would find my way back to hell and make good on my promise to Red. Then I would take it one step further. And I could bring the case before Lucifer himself. Because this shit should not be happening amongst his followers. We used our bloodlust on the humans as punishment for the ugly shit they'd done on Earth. We didn't turn on one another.

A low, mewling noise dragged me out of my swirling thoughts, making me turn to find the nurse passed out on the couch, shifting what seemed uncomfortably in her sleep.

Curious, I rose, making my way across the floor to stand near the end of the couch, looking down at her with her arm slung over the top of her head as her heavy breathing made her breasts press against the material of her tee, making her semi-hardened nipples poke out further.

I needed to walk away.

I knew it even before I felt my cock stirring again.

But I didn't take my own advice as I stood there, watching her fucking breathe for a moment before I noticed the way her back was arching a bit as she let out the noise again, as her leg slid against the couch cushion a bit rhythmically.

And I realized she wasn't making noises because she was uncomfortable.

Oh, no.

She was having some sort of sex dream.

"Mmm," she whimpered as her leg rose again, this time sliding up the back cushions until her foot planted. A low sigh escaped her as her other leg rose then hinged open, making her tee slip up, exposing her completely.

"Fuck," I hissed as desire made a sharp, stabbing sensation course through my cock as my gaze fell on her delicate pink pussy, slick with her desire.

Self-control had never been an issue for me. After this many years of life—both in hell and trapped above it—very few things felt important enough to lose my composure over.

Least of all sex.

If anything, some other so-called "sins" got harder to control the longer I'd been around.

My pride, namely.

But there was no denying that I was having zero self-control over myself twice in the span of a few hours around this woman.

It made no rational sense, either.

Yes, she was beautiful. So were millions of other women. Sure, she must have been smart and capable to do her job. And again, so were many other women.

I didn't understand my reaction to her.

Unless it was simple exhaustion and worry about Red mixed with Josephine's proximity and the fact that I hadn't gotten laid in a while.

Still, even knowing that, I didn't even try to muster the reserves of control to look away, to walk away.

I just fucking stood there. Staring at her pussy as her hips did little circles as her dream heated up. The hand above her head gripped the armrest of the couch as her back arched higher.

If she were any other woman, I would have reached down, ran my finger between her lips, worked her clit until she was screaming for release.

But she wasn't any other woman willingly, happily in our company, knowing what to expect from us.

She was a woman stolen off the street and being held captive very much against her will.

I couldn't put my hands on her.

I had no right even to stare at her in a compromised state.

Yet I didn't move away.

It was fucking Daemon that did it. Came stumbling out of his room with whatever fuck-buddy he'd brought home for the night, giggling and knocking something over in the kitchen, making Josephine's eyes snap open.

There was surprise, then panic as she tried to remember where she was, what she might be hearing.

Then her head shifted down toward the end of the couch, landed on me.

There was still some of the surprise and the panic, but it mingled with some other things right then too. Confusion, sure. But something else, something I couldn't put my finger on. It was something, though, that made me move toward her instead of away, lowering down on the armrest of the couch, making her suddenly aware of her compromised position, snapping her thighs together as her eyes went saucer round.

"Interesting dream you were having," I said, eyes roaming up her body, seeing the flush on her thighs, her neck, across her cheeks.

"I...I wasn't having a dream," she insisted, letting me know one thing about her for sure. She was an atrocious liar. Even by human standards.

"You were," I countered, sliding onto the cushion at her feet, making her scramble up slightly to give me more room.

"No."

"Your back was arching, your breathing was fast, your hips were rocking," I told her, watching her shake her head. "You were moaning," I added. "And," I went on, "your pussy was drenched."

"I, ah, no," she insisted, sounding breathless.

"Saw it myself. Want me to check to confirm?" I asked, lips curving up until I saw the way her lips parted, her breath sucked in.

"You can't."

"I can," I countered. "But only if you tell me to," I said, one fingertip teasing the inside of her ankle.

"I can't."

"You can't or won't?"

"Same thing."

"Very different," I shot back, finger tracing up the side of her calf, feeling the muscle flex under my touch.

It was right about then that Red let out a whimpering sound that made the nurse stiffen, head whipping over toward her for a moment. When she looked back at me, all the lingering desire was gone.

"Stop," she said, voice quiet, but it didn't need to be firm with that word, did it?

Pulling my hand back, I tried to deep breathe some calm back into my body as she slipped off the couch, made her way over toward Red, reaching out to touch her forehead, humming to her patient as she looked her over.

She was bending over to inspect Red's back when Daemon and his date started making noise again in the living room.

"No, come on," the woman said, laughing. "I have to get to work. You need to drive me home."

I watched as realization crossed Josephine's face.

There was someone else in the house who wasn't loyal to me, someone who could possibly save her.

Even as she was braced to run, her mouth was opening to scream.

I flew off the couch, making it in front of her as her first sound escaped her lips, my hand slapping across her mouth as I shoved her back against the wall.

"Sounds like someone else is having fun too," the woman said in the other room.

As soon as the words were said, I could feel the nurse's defeat course through her body, making the tension leave her muscles. Even so, I pressed forward, pressing my front to hers, feeling her breasts crush against me.

Her breath sucked in as my pelvis pressed to hers, making her as aware of my hard-on as I was.

My gaze held hers as my hips shifted slightly, my cock pressing just above the juncture of her thighs.

When her breath exhaled, it shook through her chest.

I knew desire when I saw it, when I felt it.

But I kept my body still, waiting for her to make the next move.

"No, stop," I heard on the other side of the door, the woman half laughing, half-serious. "Shit. That's my sister calling to make sure you didn't murder me," she added as her phone started to ring.

It was right then that Josephine jolted. Almost like she was going to fight against my hold, but oh so conveniently shifting just enough that her hips rose and my cock pressed against the heat of her.

A shiver coursed through her at the contact, her eyes going wide, her hot air exhaling hard out of her nose and over my hand still over her mouth.

Whether there was consent or not at this point was dubious at best, but my hips shifted slightly, brushing against her pussy, making a whimpering noise get muffled by my palm.

That sound, as small as it may have been, was my undoing.

Any control I'd been holding onto snapped as my free hand lowered, yanked up her leg to the side of my hip, opening her up to me as I rocked against her.

It was only maybe a minute before her hips started grinding against me, wanting more, needing release.

As I heard Daemon's bike rumble to life then pull away, I knew his girl was out of earshot, letting me drop my hand. I braced myself for her objection, for her scream, for something, anything other than the whimper that escaped her.

A low, growling noise escaped me as I felt the Change start. It was a burning sensation up my back, in my forehead where my horns threatened to push out.

Not trusting myself in that moment, I dropped suddenly down in front of her, hands sinking into her ass as I buried myself between her thighs, eating her pussy with a single-minded focus, my tongue and lips working her clit for a long moment before my hand slipped between her thighs, thrusting inside her tight pussy, feeling the walls tighten around me, pull me in.

Her hands landed on the back of my head, holding on, not pushing away, as her whimpers became moans, as her thighs started to shake.

I could feel my tongue starting to fork.

I should have stopped.

Risking exposure was against the rules.

But her fingertips dug into my skull as her hips rocked against me, getting closer, begging for release.

There was no turning back as I worked her with both sides of my tongue, hearing her throaty moans as I pushed her to the edge, then right over it, leaving her crying out, half falling forward over me, her hands slamming into my shoulders to hold her body up as her thighs shook.

Slowly, she leaned back, lowering herself down the wall even as I started to stand, the pressure of my hard cock against my pants too uncomfortable to be in that position for another moment.

Tilting my head back, I took slow, measured breaths, pulling myself back together.

My gaze lowered again when I felt my cock realize it wasn't going to get any relief, finding her crouched on the floor, looking up at me with huge eyes.

Shit.

What the fuck was I doing?

She wasn't here for me to fuck her or fuck around with her.

She was here to deal with Red.

Nothing else.

A slow, deep sigh escaped me as I tried to school my voice to adopt the cold indifference I was typically so well known for. It was harder right then than it ever had been before.

"Unless you're down there to suck me off, get your ass over there and finish taking care of your patient," I demanded, watching the emotions cross her face at a breakneck pace.

Confusion.

Shock.

Humiliation.

Then, finally, anger.

That was good, I reminded myself as she got to her feet, jaw so tight her teeth must have been aching as she slammed her shoulder against my chest to move me out of the way so she could pass. It was good that she was pissed, that she hated me.

It would keep her from reacting to me in the future.

Which would help me keep a distance.

Because eventually, and it might be sooner than either of us realized, I was going to need to kill her.

Chapter Six

Jo

What the ever-loving hell was that?

Humiliation and rage were a heady concoction coursing through me as I checked out Red's wounds, searching for any early signs of infection that would make me need to open up the stitches again.

I felt shaky and unfocused, like my body was somehow both attached to me, yet not, at the same time.

Which made sense.

Because I'd clearly misplaced my head if I had just let that happen.

I wasn't even sure if I had any right to be upset about it.

I hadn't told him no.

I hadn't fought.

I hadn't explicitly consented either, though.

Then again, when in my entire life, had any man ever *asked* before he touched me?

Never, that was when.

And when did I ever say *Yes, touch me there.*

Again, never.

Until, you know, we were already in the throws of things.

It was a gray area, I guess.

One could argue that there was no way for me to consent seeing as my presence in this situation with these people was against my will in the first place.

But there was no denying that I had wanted it. That I had even encouraged it.

God, that tongue of his.

I had no idea how I was supposed to feel about the whole situation, if I should have been angry or disgusted. All I knew was how I actually felt.

Embarrassed, because I felt like he'd somehow used me, even though he hadn't gotten any sort of satisfaction.

But also confused, because he was right. I *had* been having a sex dream. Which didn't make sense in and of itself. Then waking up and realizing that it wasn't just a subconscious thing, that I was somehow having a physical response to the man who had plucked me off the street, cuffed me, then held me against my will.

I just needed to stay the hell away from him, that was all.

It would be easier now that he'd been a complete prick, so there would be no lingering interest in feeling that tongue and those fingers again.

Then again, pricks had always been a problem for me in the past. I was chronically attracted to assholes. I thought I was in recovery for my obvious problem. Apparently not.

"How is she?" a female voice asked softly what felt like ages later, making me turn to find the woman from the night before—Lenore—standing in the doorway holding a pile of something in her hands.

"It's a little soon to tell," I admitted. "But if she doesn't get infected in the next day or two, I think we can breathe a sigh of relief," I told her, shaking another antibiotic into my hand, then quickly pushing it down the woman's throat.

"She's not screaming."

No, she wasn't. But I had the strangest feeling that while she wasn't doing it outwardly, that she was somehow screaming on the inside. I had no way of backing that belief up, but I couldn't shake it either. There was just something about the way she writhed, the way her eyelids fluttered, the way her lip trembled.

"The pain medicine works wonders," I told her.

"How is your head?" she asked. "From where you hit it," she clarified when I stared at her blankly.

After washing the gunk off in the shower, I honestly hadn't given it another thought. My hand rose automatically, touching what felt like sealed skin.

"Ah, it feels alright. How does it look?" I asked.

"It's healing," she told me. "That poultice has never failed my people. It works wonders. You have a bruise here though," she said, rubbing under her eye.

"I think I have a concussion," I admitted, though I was doing so to try to convince myself that maybe it was a factor in my unusual behavior even if I knew it really had nothing to do with it.

"I don't know what that means," Lenore admitted, shrugging. "But I hope it doesn't hurt."

"No. I mean it did. But sleep helped," I told her. "Well, I only got a little bit of sleep. I was woken up."

"By Red?" she asked, gaze slipping toward the bed.

"No."

"Oh," she said, pressing her lips together. "Um, Ace can be a bit..."

"Of an asshole," I supplied.

"Yeah, that," Lenore said, sharing a knowing smile with me. "But he did ask me to bring you clothes. And a blanket. I also set out a toothbrush for you in the bathroom. I will be making some breakfast soon. The men don't usually eat with me."

"Why not?"

"Something about how I eat twigs and leaves," she said, rolling her eyes. "I don't eat flesh," she added.

"Oh, okay. Well, that's fine. I don't need meat," I agreed, feeling the gnawing of my stomach. I would eat whatever I could get.

"I don't think I'm allowed to bring you out of the room, but I will bring you some when I finish making it. And then maybe Lycus can come in here and bring you to the bathroom and such," she said, giving me a small smile before handing me the pile of clothes and blankets, and heading out.

She'd brought me a floor-length canary yellow dress and a sweater that I quickly slipped on, feeling I needed the layers even if I was not exactly a dress-wearing sort of woman, finding the long skirts more problematic than pants since I was so short and they always dragged across the ground, getting filthy or trapped under my feet.

The rest of that day was relatively uneventful.

Lenore brought me a breakfast of oatmeal with fresh fruit and honey. I was maybe a bit of a Pops or Cinnamon Toast Crunch sort of girl, to be honest, but it was edible, and it proved to be the only meal I got until dinner, so I was glad I choked it down.

Lycus, who turned out to be Lenore's man, showed up sometime after to escort me to the bathroom, but let me close the door all the way for some privacy.

He, Aram, and some grumpy, angry-looking giant named Bael helped me temporarily move Red so we could get fresh sheets on the bed to help keep her wounds clean.

I gave Red her pain medicine and another dose of antibiotics. I checked her temperature and her wounds. I hummed to her to try to ease whatever hell she was going through on the inside.

Then, eventually, exhaustion pulling at my eyelids, I dragged myself back to the couch, curling up under the blanket Lenore had provided even though the house was too hot already. I just wanted the protection when I wasn't conscious.

Eventually, sleep claimed me.

It was a voice that woke me up some indeterminate time later.

Low, soothing.

The creaking hinge is oiled,
I have unbarred the backway,
But you tread not the trackway;
And shall the thing be spoiled?

I slow blinked in the mostly dark room, the only light coming from the low bulb in the nightstand lamp.

Ace was lounging there in a fold-up chair he must have brought in with him, a small book open in his lap, his gaze fixed on it as he recited the poem.

Far cockcrows echo shrill,
The shadows are abating,
And I am waiting, waiting;
But, O, you tarry still.

I'll admit, I had never really been a poetry fan. I mean, sure, I went through my Edgar Allen Poe phase like any teenaged girl who thought his doomed love poetry was the ultimate in romance, but aside from *Annabel Lee* and *The Raven*, I'd never really taken to verse. Not even when I'd dated a very sensitive guy in high school who dragged me to some run-down coffee house that hosted slam poetry readings in a back room.

I always found them hard to follow, especially the older poems with more archaic wording.

But, somehow, with the calm, confident, and gentle way Ace was reciting this one, it was oddly hypnotic.

"What is that?" I heard myself ask before I even realized I was going to ask.

Ace's head lifted, his cool blue gaze on me for a long moment before answering. "Thomas Hardy."

"What's the poem?" I asked, suddenly wanting to know how it started.

"*I say I'll Seek Her*," he supplied.

"It's pretty," I decided, feeling lame for not having anything else to say about it.

"Hardy was a romantic," he said, and even though I wasn't sure I fully understood his meaning, it sounded like he was agreeing with me to an extent, which made me feel a little less silly.

"It's good to talk to them," I supplied, folding up to a seated position, pulling the blanket up to my shoulders. "When patients seem lost in their own heads," I clarified. "It's good to talk to them. A lot of people who wake up even from comas say they could hear things, but just couldn't wake up. Does she like poetry?" I asked.

"I don't know."

"Isn't she your friend?"

"Yeah."

"You never asked?"

"Do your friends ask if you like dead poets?" he shot back.

It was probably not a good idea to let him know that I didn't really have any friends. Any family. Any significant other. Anyone who would notice I was missing, would look for me.

"I guess not," I said, shrugging.

Ace's attention went to Red, then back to me. "We are going to need to move her," he said, mostly to himself.

"We moved her earlier," I told him. "To change the sheets," I clarified.

"I meant in a car."

"To a hospital?"

"No."

"She shouldn't be moved. She's... she's covered in wounds. If you're not careful, the stitches will open up."

"Well, then you will need to stitch them up again," he said, rising, making his way to the door.

It certainly sounded like he planned to bring me with them.

"Where are you going?"

"*We* are going home," he told me, strolling out and closing the door before I could ask anything else.

I was left alone to contemplate his words.

I guess I thought they were home. It was certainly someone's home we were in. If it was not theirs, then why were they here? Where was home?

My stomach clenched at the idea of being dragged anywhere else, but I was also not naive enough to think I had any sort of control over the situation. Not with so many men in the house.

Ace, Lycus, Aram, Seven, Drex, Bael, and the guy Daemon that I hadn't seen but had heard. Plus Lenore. I was more than outnumbered. If they wanted to take me somewhere, they could and would. And, really, the only control I had was over not getting myself too hurt in the process.

Maybe, if we were changing locations, it would give me a chance to come across some other people who might help me.

Whatever the move was, it didn't happen that day.

Not the day after that, either.

It wasn't until the third day that I was startled awake by a small group of the men as they burst into the room, flicking on the overhead light, leaving me with a frantic heartbeat, trying to force my eyes to adjust to the brightness.

"What's the matter?" I asked, clutching my blanket tighter to my chest.

"We're heading out," Aram supplied, being the one who seemed to take more sympathy on me.

"Heading out where?"

"Home," Ace snapped. "Like I told you."

"Where is home?" I pressed.

"I can't imagine why you would need to know that," he told me as he made his way toward the bed, looking down at Red. "Come over here and get her ready to go."

"She shouldn't be moved," I snapped at him, throwing off the blanket to stalk across the floor. "She's still barely healing."

"Yeah, well, we waited as long as possible," he told me. "So do what you can. Because we are leaving within the hour," he said as the other men grabbed things out of the closets, the dressers, shoving them into suitcases.

With little choice, I did a quick cleanse of the wounds with saline, dried her, then gently wrapped as much of her in gauze as possible, hoping to minimize any tearing during the transport.

I gave her another pain pill, then turned to find Ace watching me, arms folded over his chest. "That's the best I can do," I told him, shaking my head.

"Good. Aram, get Bael and Ly," he said. "We are going to carry her on the sheet like a makeshift stretcher. "You, get over here," he demanded, daring me to object.

I wanted to tell him to go screw himself, but I also understood that not ending up hurt was in my best interest. I needed to be sharp. I didn't need another concussion.

So with gritted teeth, I moved toward him, figuring it out a moment too late what he intended to do.

Because my wrists were encircled in cuffs in what felt like two seconds.

It wasn't in my best interest to antagonize him, but his cold, indifferent arrogance just rubbed me the wrong way. I couldn't seem to keep control of my runaway mouth.

"That's fine. I can still scream," I said, shrugging.

"No," he told me, but the word was strangely soft, almost apologetic.

I didn't understand it until his hand lifted, and I felt a sharp pinch stab into my shoulder.

I looked down to see the needle sticking out of my arm for a second before the wooziness swirled through me, making me feel like I was floating, like I was half-asleep in seconds.

I swayed on my feet, and Ace's hands went around me, pulling me to his body, my face resting against his chest.

I could have sworn he whispered *Sorry* before I drifted off.

But, no, that wasn't possible.

Men like him never apologized for anything.

They had too much pride.

But soon I was unconscious.

And nothing mattered.

Chapter Seven

Ace

It was a fucking miserable ride back home.

Daemon and Bael took off first with Drex, Seven, and Aram, getting a head start on their bikes while the rest of us piled into the SUV with Red and Josephine unconscious in the back, our own bikes in a trailer.

We couldn't stay another day, even if I was more worried about moving Red than I would let on. The house was a rental. And they had another client coming to stay in two days.

We had to clear out with plenty of notice.

Especially when we were traveling with a fucking hostage.

I should have taken her out to the woods and done away with her, but had somehow convinced myself that Red might need her on the long ride home.

It was something like a thirty-five-hour drive back from Utah. But I'd convinced Lycus, and Minos to drive it in shifts so we didn't have to stay over anywhere.

There was a lot of bad that could happen with Red's condition from our start to end points. And I'd reasoned that it was easier to transport Josephine with us than to possibly have to abduct someone else halfway through the trip.

It had been Drex's idea to drug the nurse to keep her from drawing attention to us. I'd had no good argument against it, even if, for some reason, I didn't like the idea.

I took the first leg of the drive while Minos slept in the passenger seat and Ly and Lenore slept together in the middle row.

We stopped eight hours later when the nurse started to rouse. We'd pulled up to a gas station that had a detached bathroom, backing up to it, and helping a groggy Josephine out, letting Lenore take her inside.

"Please don't," she said, gaze finding mine in the mirror as I walked in behind her as Lenore moved outside again. "I don't feel good."

"This will help that," I told her, pulling out the second needle.

"Ace, please," she begged, eyes getting glassy. "I won't scream," she said as a tear fell down. "I don't like not knowing what's going on."

"Nothing is going on," I assured her. "One person is driving. Everyone else is sleeping. Including you," I told her, sticking the needle in her arm before I could think any better of it.

I felt bad doing it to her the first time when she had no idea what was going to happen.

I felt a fuck of a lot worse doing it the second time, when she did, when she pleaded for it not to happen again.

But, I tried to comfort myself, it wasn't going to hurt her. It was just to knock her out for a couple hours.

The first time, so I could drive.

The second time, so I could sleep.

Maybe after she got up the next time, I could keep her quiet without the drugs.

"How is she?" I asked Lenore as she fussed over Red while I shuffled Josephine in beside her.

"From what I can tell, she's okay. I gave her more of her antibiotic," she said, shrugging.

"She's not bleeding anywhere?"

"Not that I can see. I will keep an eye on her while you sleep," she said, giving me a small smile as we both climbed into the backseat with Minos and Ly in the front.

The next eight hours, I was dead to the world, the exhaustion from the past few nights weighing down on me.

"Ace," Lenore called, waking me.

"What?" I asked, slow-blinking into the darkness. "What's the matter?"

"She's crying."

"Red?" I asked, rubbing my dry eyes.

"No."

I was awake and turned over the backseat in a blink, finding Josephine curled on her side, knees to chest, palms pressed to her eyes.

"Minos, we need to stop," I called, climbing over the backseat to wedge myself in the minuscule space between the nurse and Red. "What's the matter?" I asked, reaching out to press a hand to the back of her neck, feeling her tacky skin, wondering if Drex had fucked up the dose.

"I don't feel good," she said, whimpering. "What was it?" she asked.

I didn't need to ask to know what she was asking. What did I drug her with?

I just knew she wasn't going to like the answer. Hell, I didn't like the answer. But Drex assured me it was the only thing I could give her with an injection that he could get from one of the MCs in that area.

"It doesn't matter," I told her. "It should be wearing off. You'll feel better in a little bit." I hoped. Really, I knew nothing about it. Sure, we provided all sorts of party drugs when we threw events at our place. But I'd always drawn the line at this kind of shit. The "make her forget what happened" shit.

"My heart feels like it is beating out of my chest," she told me, making me reach out toward her throat, pressing my fingers in.

"It's not. You're panicking."

"Gee," she said, sniffling hard. "I wonder why. It's not like my kidnapper injected me with some unknown drug or anything."

I didn't engage with that because she was right. It was a shitty thing to do. I figured, though, if she knew the choice was ketamine in her system or dead in the woods, she would choose being in a bad K-hole over a grave any day of the week.

"We will get some food in you," I said. "Some coffee. You'll feel better."

"Until you inject me again," she whimpered, rocking back and forth, trying to comfort herself.

"I won't do it again."

"Right. Because you're so trustworthy."

I couldn't expect her to trust me. If there was one thing I'd noticed about humans the past fifty years or so, it was that they didn't trust anyone. Even if the other person hadn't given them a reason to be so distrustful.

Meanwhile, I'd kidnapped her, held her hostage, manipulated her physically, and now I'd drugged her.

Her anger was understandable, if inconvenient.

We didn't plan on any stops aside from fueling up.

Getting Red home was of the utmost importance.

The other guys would be several days behind us, not having the option of shift driving, but they would hit up a couple MC chapters along the way, friends we'd made over time, and secure more supplies we might need for Red going forward.

We needed to get back as soon as possible.

But it wouldn't do us much good if the nurse overdosed on the way back.

"Alright. Lenore and I will take her to the bathroom to clean up," I said, nodding toward the detached bathroom at the rest stop. "You go get her some food and coffee," I told Minos, the one of us who knew most about feeding the humans since he'd been in charge of feeding all the witches when they came to us as sacrifices over the years.

"Got it," he agreed as we parked, leaving Ly with the SUV and Red as we all went off on our separate ways.

Lenore was in the bathroom with the nurse for fifteen minutes before they emerged again, Josephine leaning heavily on Lenore.

"She's dizzy," Lenore supplied. "And a little confused," she added as I took her other arm.

"Confused how?"

"She asked me who I was twice."

"Alright. Can you get in the back with Red for a while?" I asked. "She needs someone to keep an eye on her. You know more than the rest of us."

"Okay," she agreed, letting me help Josephine into the backseat where she groaned, her hand pressing to her stomach, then leaned over into my shoulder, resting her head against me.

"I'm spinning."

"You're not," I clarified, grabbing her arm to ground her. I couldn't count how many times I'd seen people get shitfaced at one of our parties, leaving them laying flat on the floor to shake off the overheated sensation, arms and legs thrown out to touch walls or tables, trying to assure themselves that they weren't, in fact, spinning.

"I am," she objected, letting out a whining noise as she pressed her head harder against me.

She was so short that her feet dangled just above the ground, making me grab her legs, draping them over mine to make her feel more stable.

"You're nice," she declared, snuggling closer.

"I'm not," I told her. "I'm really not," I added as I saw Minos making his way out of the fast food place.

It never really occurred to me to give a shit if I was decent or not. That wasn't exactly my nature, was it? But I'd been finding that the longer we were all trapped here, the more we became aware and even concerned by our lack of humanity. It appeared in small ways sometimes even years apart, so it got easy to forget it was a growing problem.

The last time I remembered giving a shit about humans was when the guys and I were on a run to a biker meetup in Florida and we happened by a fresh car wreck.

Everything in our nature should have told us to keep going. It wasn't our problem. We weren't supposed to give a shit if there were humans screaming for help inside of their totaled cars that had caught fire in the engine.

Yet we'd all stopped in unison. We'd worked to free them. We'd waited until the paramedics showed up. And only then were we off again.

Before that, I remembered a kid being taken from its mother while she was looking away. I'd stepped in then as well.

And before that, shit, I didn't even know.

But none of it, according to our nature, should have ever happened.

There was no denying that as time went on, we adopted human ways as our own in many ways. It was changing how we reacted to certain situations, to the humans themselves.

I knew, as a leader, as the oldest, that it was dangerous. It could impact our small, but important role on this plane. Bringing the humans' innate evilness to the surface so they acted on it more readily. If we cared too much about them, could we continue to do that? If we somehow felt like we couldn't, what did that say about us, as creatures of hell? Were we no longer as evil? Would we not be able to go back home, to take over our old jobs, our only reason for existence?

It was important to separate ourselves from the humans and their many pesky emotions.

Still, as I sat there with this near stranger of a woman draped over me, trying to steal some strength and stability from me, there was no denying I was giving a shit.

Guilt was not an emotion I remembered personally feeling in the past. Yet I'd felt that way several times just since I'd come in contact with this woman.

It didn't make any sense to me.

And not knowing things, that never sat well with me.

"Ugh, no," Josephine groaned when I tried to get her to eat.

"You'll feel better."

"I'll throw up," she told me, and Minos snatched back the bag so fast I barely caught the motion.

"We're in a moving car," he grumbled. "I'm not getting stuck in here with vomit. Deal with that shit enough at the parties."

That was fair enough. There was never a house party we hosted that didn't end up with one of us hosing down the back patio or scrubbing one of the bathrooms.

Humans and their weak stomachs.

"Alright," I said, reaching for the coffee. "Try this then," I said, holding it up to her lips when she refused to reach for it. Because one of her hands was tucked behind me, and the other was somewhat obsessively tracing the stubble that had grown on my face without me noticing.

"Gross," she grumbled, but took a couple more sips before resting her head against me again.

"You should sleep."

"Mmhmm," she agreed, sounding halfway there already.

"What?" I asked, seeing Minos shooting me a look over his shoulder as Josephine passed out, arm draped across my waist.

"I didn't say anything."

"What's the look for then?"

"This just looks really familiar."

"What? Like with you and your claimed woman?" I snapped, still more annoyed than I had a right to be over something I understood he and Ly could not control. I had no idea who Minos's woman was, but I knew she existed. I knew she rejected him. And I knew it had irreparably changed him ever since.

"No," he said, sighing out his breath as a mask came down over his face. "Reminds me of Ly and Lenore," he clarified before turning forward, and putting on some of that sad sack music he liked so much these days. *Music to slit your wrists to* was what I'd heard Drex describe it as, and it wasn't too far off the mark.

I wanted to shake off his comment, but as the hours dragged on, as Josephine climbed all over me like a fucking cat in her sleep until I wound up cradling her on my lap, my arms around her so she didn't go flying when we braked or took a turn, I couldn't stop them from swirling around my head at a break-neck pace.

See, I'd missed the signs with Ly. I guess because Claiming was rare with our kind. And after Minos went through it, I thought that would be it for us.

But in the weeks after I realized what had happened under my nose, I'd started to analyze that time when Lenore came out of our basement and found her way into Ly's world.

Minos wasn't completely off.

Because Ly had always been hard and rough and even cruel at times. But there had been a softness with

Lenore I'd never seen with him before. And if I were being perfectly honest, I was starting to see some of that same shit with the nurse. Even after just a couple days.

It wasn't just because after I'd gotten a taste of her, practically half of my thoughts were consumed with burying my cock inside her. Though there was that too.

It was this kind of shit.

She should have been in the back, sleeping off another dose of the ketamine. Because it shouldn't have mattered if she was in a k-hole. It shouldn't have mattered that she felt like shit. Because, she was not a permanent fixture in our lives. She was here for a job. And then she was going to be disposed of.

That thought, though, it made a strange, sharp sensation pierce my chest.

At some point, I found myself passing back out as well, waking up when Ly announced we were almost home to Josephine draped over me, her face nuzzled into my neck, her hand placed over my heart, her legs resting on either side of me.

Clearly, I'd been feeling her wiggle against me because I woke up with a painfully throbbing cock pressing between her spread thighs. That skirt of her dress had ridden up to allow her legs to go on either side of me, and since Lenore's kind didn't believe in undergarments, that meant Josephine's pussy was as bare as it had been the last time I was close to her.

Without meaning to, my hips shifted up slightly, pressing against her, dragging a sleepy sigh out of her.

My gaze shifted toward the front, finding Minos leaning against the window, passed out. Behind me, Lenore seemed asleep as well. Ly's focus was on the road. And Minos's whiny music was still playing loudly enough through the speakers.

I was a real fuck for crossing the line again, but I couldn't make myself give a shit as I jerked my hips upward against her again, waking her up with the sensation.

She didn't respond at first, likely still out of sorts from the drugs leaving her system and from sleep.

My hips ground upward again, getting a quiet gasp at her as she pushed up slightly, looking down at me with those sleepy brown eyes that were a mix of confused and heated.

My hands slid down her back, sank into her ass, grinding her down onto me, watching as her lips opened on a silent moan as a shiver racked her system.

She didn't pull away.

She didn't say no.

No, instead, she did another little wiggle with her hips.

That was all I needed.

I used her ass to grind her against me as I thrust upward, finding the rhythm that made her breathing go fast and shallow, made her muscles tense, made it impossible for her to keep her sounds in.

My hand went to the back of her neck, pressing her face hard against my shoulder to muffle her sounds as I drove her up, then over the edge, feeling her body shudder as a throaty moan vibrated against my shirt.

She didn't move after, just clung to me as aftershocks racked her system. Satisfied. While my cock was still throbbing for release.

Don't get me wrong, if you weren't getting the woman you were with off too, I didn't see the point. But I don't remember the last time I walked away from a sexual encounter with a woman and didn't finish myself.

Now I'd fucked around with this woman twice. *Twice*. And I got nothing out of it.

What the fuck was going on with me?

"We're here," Lycus called, making Minos jolt as he startled awake. Behind us, I could see Lenore sitting up as well.

Taking a steadying breath, I folded upward, pushing Josephine off my lap, trying to bring some calm back into my system.

"I'll come back for Red," I snapped, grabbing Josephine around the wrist, and dragging her out of the car with me, up the drive, through the front door, and upstairs.

To Red's room.

I wanted her in mine.

And that was exactly why she couldn't be.

I needed to get some distance from this woman.

Because I got the distinct feeling that something was going to happen if I didn't. Something similar to what had happened with Minos and Lycus.

And that couldn't fucking happen.

Chapter Eight

Jo

They lived in a mansion.

I don't know why that was so shocking to me, but as Ace practically dragged me out of the car, I couldn't help but feel a little bit in awe of the massive gray stone house with its abundance of windows, its utter privacy on a giant piece of land with a whole forest around it.

Perfectly secluded.

Which didn't bode well for me, did it?

But I didn't let my mind drift there as Ace unlocked the front door and pulled me inside, his hand biting into my wrist that was barely starting to lose the bruises from the cuffs from that first night.

I tried to tell myself that I was fascinated by the home because I was trying to learn the layout so that I could possibly find a way to escape one day or night when everyone was occupied.

The fact of the matter was, though, that I'd grown up really poor. I was accustomed to cheap apartments in bad neighborhoods where nothing was ever quiet, not even in the middle of the night when I was trying to sleep. I was used to thrift store furniture with holes and burn marks and weird odors that never quite came out, no matter how much dollar store perfume my mother doused it with.

And while I'd done decently well for myself as an adult, choosing a steady career that paid relatively well, especially for a single woman, I had never seen actual grandeur up close and personal.

It was like touring a celebrity's house. Without any of the actual pointing out of things as Ace dragged me right up the front staircase, giving me only a brief look inside what seemed to be a library—which made sense since Ace clearly liked books—and what seemed to be a kitchen toward the back of the house.

There had been lush Oriental rugs lining the hallway, looking expensive and soft, but I didn't get to test that theory out for myself as Ace kept up the breakneck pace up the stairs, seeming to forget—or simply not caring—that my legs were a lot shorter than his, so every step he took was two for me.

On top of that, I was still not quite right after he'd dosed me the second time.

I'd dealt with a decent amount of overdoses in my line of work, unfortunately. I knew a bad trip when I was experiencing one. And judging by the fact that he shot me up instead of shoved a pill down my throat, I felt relatively safe in assuming it had been ketamine. One of the several date-rape type drugs.

I didn't want to consider why he had access to such things.

Clearly, he didn't need them to coerce me into forgetting myself and letting him do things with me.

That wasn't quite fair, though, was it?

There had been no coercion. He'd given me ample time to object. I just hadn't. And I couldn't even begin to wrap my head around why that was.

Sure, I had a normal, healthy sex drive.

And, yes, he was an attractive man.

But that had never been enough for me to completely forget myself and let someone bring me to orgasm in a public sort of setting.

What the hell was that about?

Maybe now that we were at a permanent location, I would have some time and space to work through my swirling, uncomfortable thoughts.

For God's sake, I didn't even know where we were. I should have been focusing on trying to figure that out, not letting my freaking captor put his hands on me.

"Here," Ace snapped, practically tossing me inside a bedroom, making me stumble, needing to grab the side of the four-poster bed to steady myself.

"What? You're not going to nail the windows shut?" I asked, shooting daggers at him.

"If you would like to fling yourself out of a two-story window, be my guest," he said, tone biting.

And with that, he moved back out, slamming the door.

I didn't imagine this was my chance to escape, so I took a couple deep breaths before looking around the room.

I imagined this was Red's bedroom judging by the more feminine look to it from the toss pillows on the bed to the green tufted velvet couch under a set of the massive windows that, as Ace suggested, did lead to quite a drop. The kind of drop that would break all the bones in your legs if it didn't outright kill you.

So that was out.

Trying not to feel defeated, I moved into the attached bathroom, finding bright white everything. Including a deep soaking tub.

Everything was neat. No personal touches were lying around. So I guess Red was a tidy person.

I had at least half a dozen things on my sink vanity at any given time. I always told myself I would be one of those people who put things away as they used it, but it never happened.

There were voices down the hall, then inside the bedroom as they brought in Red.

"How is she?" I asked, looking at Lenore, hoping she'd been keeping an eye on her while I'd been incapacitated.

"She seems okay," Lenore supplied, pulling down the comforter so the men could slip Red onto the bed.

"I'll grab the supplies," Ace announced, making his way toward the door, seeming to hug the other wall simply to be as far from me as possible.

"You gonna look her over?" Lycus asked, snapping my attention back to him.

"Of course," I agreed. "You all can go," I added. "I imagine Red would appreciate her privacy," I told them.

The poor woman had been nearly, if not completely, nude around these men for days. Even the most confident women I knew didn't let it all hang out around male friends. If that was what these people were to her. I didn't even know. I didn't understand their dynamic.

There had been motorcycles and leather jackets.

I couldn't claim to know much of anything about them, but I figured they had a motorcycle club of some sort. Which explained their willingness to kidnap and steal, I guess.

"I'm fucking beat," Ly said, dropping an arm on his woman's shoulders. "Come keep me company," he added, pulling her along with him.

"If you need anything, we are two doors down," Lenore told me, giving me a smile before she was led away.

"You need food, right?" Minos asked, reaching up to pull his long hair into a bun. "We got you food at the last stop but you didn't want to eat."

My stomach had felt like someone was wringing it out back then. But now? I was famished.

"I'm starving," I agreed. "Thank you," I added.

Aside from Aram who was nowhere around, I had the best feeling about Minos. And I figured it wasn't a bad thing for me to get on the better side of at least a few of these people.

Minos said nothing as he moved out of the room, closing the door behind him.

Alone, I moved toward Red, pulling down the sheet, checking her wounds, feeling for her pulse and temperature. Aside from a few spots on her back that looked a little red, likely from moving around in the car, she was looking pretty good. All things considered.

Once I had the supplies, I would give her another saline rinse and another dose of her medicine. But in another day or two, we could probably ease her back on the pain medicine. She was on a heavy dose, and it might have been the reason she was still so out of it, lost in her own head.

I now knew a thing or two about being drugged. And getting to the surface of your consciousness felt a hell of a lot like swimming through molasses. Red hadn't gotten a break from the drugs yet—for good reason, her pain would have been excruciating—but as soon as we could, we needed to give her the chance to surface again.

"That's everything for now," Ace's voice startled me, making me turn to find him dropping a bag on the couch. "You stay in here."

With that, he was gone, closing the door.

I figured that was it until about fifteen minutes later when I heard drilling. Then the slide of a chain on the other side of the door.

So that was that.

Unless one of them was coming in to check on Red or bring me food, I was locked in.

After a couple hours of pacing the bedroom, I was seriously starting to contemplate tying together all the bedding and clothes in Red's closet to scale down out the window like some prison movie.

In the end, though, I'd raided Red's closet, intent on taking a shower, then getting some rest.

The only problem was that Red was the kind of woman I was convinced was the figment of male movie makers' minds, not one who actually existed. She was the kind of woman who didn't own a single pair of "comfy" PJs. Oh, no. She was the sort of woman who favored lace and silk. All of it short and tight.

Her day clothes were similar. Tight jeans, short skirts, tops that were heavy on the cleavage spillage and skintight.

On a sigh, I stole some of her panties and a burgundy silk tank and shorts set that was lined in black lace. It was entirely too sexy. But it was clean. And that was really all that mattered after being in the same dress for days.

So I showered, going ahead and using all of Red's various beauty products, then took one of the many blankets from the closet—wondering all the while what these peoples' obsession was with warmth—and climbed onto the couch to sleep, at least a little comforted by the locked door.

See, the problem with locked doors was they could be unlocked.

When you were unconscious and vulnerable and unaware.

I woke up slowly, sleep stubbornly clinging to my thoughts, leaving me laying there with closed eyes, lulled a bit by a low timbre of a man's voice in the room. It took a solid minute or two before I realized that what I was hearing was not what I wanted to hear.

Ace's voice.

In the same room as me.

My eyes snapped open, slow-blinking into the darkness of the room, finding the source of the voice.

Ace was sitting in a brown leather barrel chair that hadn't been in the room when I'd gone to sleep. He'd changed into a pair of gray sweatpants and a black hoodie, despite the thermostat likely being set around eighty.

He had a book open in his hands, one much thicker than the last one.

At last I put off love,
For twice ten years...

I wanted to hate the man.

He'd certainly earned my derision.

But I found myself captivated by the smooth sound of his voice, the confident, familiar way his mouth moved over the words.

My eyes drifted closed again, wanting him to think I was still asleep so I could listen to him read for a while longer.

I didn't pretend to understand my reaction to him.

I didn't even get my apparent newfound interest in old poetry.

There was just something hypnotic about the way he recited the poems—with a sort of reverence I found myself inexplicably drawn to.

"Are you done pretending you're asleep?" Ace asked, making me jolt at the sudden change in tone.

His reading voice was smooth and soothing.

The voice he used on me was sharp, cutting.

Like he was annoyed with me.

With me!

Meanwhile, I was the one ripped off the street, cuffed, injured, held captive, used, and drugged.

The bastard.

"I was hoping you would shut up and leave," I told him, sitting up, my chin jerking up.

"Dressed up for me to tell me to fuck off?" he asked, closing his book as his gaze raked over my exposed skin. And there was a lot of it, thanks to Red's signature style.

"For your information, Red seems to be allergic to cotton and comfy," I told him, confused and annoyed by the way the skin his gaze moved over felt suddenly warm and sensitive. I was sure that if I looked down, I would find a flush over my chest and neck. So I went ahead and didn't look down. I didn't need proof of how screwed up I was about this whole situation, and this man in particular.

He ignored that, likely knowing it was true.

"No riveting commentary about the poem selection tonight? Were they, perhaps, *pretty*?" he asked, not even trying to pretend he wasn't mocking me, throwing my own words back in my face.

"Why are you such an asshole?" I snapped, too annoyed to care about keeping the peace, not provoking my captor. "I mean, where do you get off being so nasty? Were you the one kidnapped, held against your will, and drugged? If you find me so inconvenient, you can let me go. I will even let my damn self out," I said, flicking off the blanket, and making my way toward the door.

It wasn't like I thought he would actually let me go.

I was just sick of being a good little captive while he made me miserable and confused.

My hand barely even closed around the doorknob before I heard a growling noise—so animalistic-sounding that I felt my heart leap in my chest—a second before a hand slammed into the door above my head as another hand grabbed the back of my neck, yanking me backward, forcefully turning me. His hand slid around my neck to my throat, slamming me back against the door by it.

"Don't fucking test me," he demanded, voice rougher than I'd heard it.

And his eyes.

His eyes didn't seem so blue anymore.

They seemed red.

But no.

That didn't make any sense.

People didn't get red eyes.

It was just a trick of the light.

I swallowed hard.

Because I was supposed to be terrified.

Why, then, was there something else coursing through my system? Something warm and liquid, something that made my nerve endings feel like they were humming, something that made me very much aware of an oppressive weight on my lower stomach?

"Or what?" I heard myself asking the question like I was suddenly outside my body, watching on as some weird, bold, daring version of myself decided to try to go toe-to-toe with her captor.

"You should keep your mouth shut, Josephine," he told me, my name sounding way too good rolling off of his tongue. "Or I will find some other use for it," he added.

It was a threat.

Yet my sex tightened at the sound of it.

"You said you wouldn't force me," I reminded him, head feeling a little swimmy with the pressure of his fingertips on each side of my throat.

"You think I'd need to force you?" he challenged, hand sliding to my shoulder, pushing until I started to go down on my knees.

I knew I was going to hate myself for it, but my hands rose, grabbed the front of his pants, and started drawing them down.

I had no idea, though, just how much I was going to be disgusted with myself when his hand suddenly grabbed my chin, fingers digging in.

"Told you," he said, eyes as cold as his voice.

And with that, he yanked his pants back into place, sidestepped me, and made his way out of the room, closing, and locking the door.

Leaving me there on the floor feeling pathetic and rejected.

Which was fitting, I guessed.

Because I had been pathetic.

What the hell was going on with me? Why would I want someone who had treated me like he did?

Maybe it was something primal.

There was no denying Ace was extremely alpha, dominant, the leader of this group of men and women. As such, he had all the pride and arrogance that came with that position.

And maybe some long-buried, cave woman part of me responded to that, recognized that his would be virile genes, that he would be a fierce protector.

That was why women—smart, educated, mature women—often found themselves with hot bad boy loser sorts, wasn't it?

It was chemical.

Not personal.

I could come to terms with that. I could even, now that I recognized it for what it was, avoid it in the future.

At least that was the plan.

Because the last man in the world I could ever actually want—on more than a physical level—was that grandpa-sweater-wearing, poetry reading, egotistical, asshole.

I mean the man's eyes went crazy when he was annoyed. If that wasn't a red flag, I didn't know what was.

And, sure, I clearly had a track record of liking jackasses.

But I was trying to be a better person.

Whether or not my lady business wanted to agree with me.

Desire was mind over matter, right? That was why as soon as your boyfriend became your ex, you were disgusted by the idea of them touching you again.

I just needed to remind myself to be disgusted by Ace.

It proved easier than I thought because for the next three days, I didn't see Ace.

He came in every night to read to Red, but I pretended to be asleep, and he didn't call me out again.

I mean, his voice was still like liquid sex, but when those thoughts came up, I ran the highlights of his assholeness across my mind. It helped.

As did the physical distance.

Until I all but forgot the attraction was there anymore.

Eventually, the other men rumbled up the driveway.

Drex came in to replenish the supplies, casting curious glances at Red who had been weaned down on the pain medicine, but still showed no signs of coming back to the world.

I didn't say—namely because no one asked—but I was really starting to worry about her. Not so much on a physical level. She was healing, slowly but surely. But mentally, emotionally. I couldn't think of a reason she was still trapped inside her mind. Other than the psychological impact of the events that left her whipped, beaten, and horribly injured.

That kind of thing was enough to cause some sort of psychological break. I mean, I couldn't claim to be an expert in that field, but I'd seen several assault victims come in very much shut down to have their kits done and wounds treated.

I hadn't even been able to do a kit on Red. If anything like that had happened. Even if it hadn't, the damage she'd endured everywhere else was more than enough to traumatize her.

It was the night after the other men returned home that I woke up to a different type of voice in the room.

Ace's, but not the slow, comforting timbre he used when he recited poetry to Red. This was a pained, desperate tone I'd never heard from him before.

"You've got to fucking wake up, Red," he demanded.

I slit my eyes to look over at him, finding him with his usual poetry book in his hands, but leaning his arms on the bed beside her, his shoulders slumped, his head hanging.

"I need to know who did this." The way he said it made me believe that he wanted to know not because he wanted to report them to the authorities, but because he planned to take justice into his own hands.

I'd never been a fan of vigilante justice. I'd seen too many instances of people being ugly with each other in the hospitals I'd worked at. But just this once, I was pretty sure I could condone an eye-for-an-eye sort of vengeance.

I'd never seen anyone as badly abused as Red had been.

Someone needed to pay for that.

It would feel like the scales were tipped toward evil in the world until that happened.

"This never should have fucking happened," he added, voice rough. "I'm supposed to take care of you all."

I didn't want to feel bad for him.

But there was a rawness in his tone that I hadn't heard before. And some part of me responded to it.

Because, clearly, he felt responsible in some way or another. Because he was their leader. Because he thought it was his job to protect them all. And she'd been horribly abused without him being able to stop it.

It wasn't his fault, of course. People did wicked things every single day, and no amount of love and protection could help at times. Wicked things happened because wicked people existed. No one has any control over that.

"It wasn't your fault," I said, wincing, knowing I was breaking my rules about not talking to him, not connecting with him in any way.

Ace's head shifted, gaze finding me.

I saw the pain there that I'd heard in his voice.

"You don't know what you're talking about." There was a hint of that condescension I had begun to associate with him, but it sounded more forced than usual.

"Did you whip her?" I asked, folding up on the couch.

"No."

"Did you hold her down while someone else did? Did you stand by and do nothing while they did that to her?"

"No."

"Then it's not your fault. People are evil sometimes," I told him, shrugging. "There's nothing we can do about that. And beating yourself up over it isn't going to change what happened."

"I'm not looking to change what happened," he told me, rising. "I'm looking to peel the skin off the bastards who did this," he told me, tone icy as he made his way across the room toward the door.

The scariest thing, though, was the fact that I felt like he meant every word. Not only did he mean them, but I absolutely thought he was capable of something that horrific.

It wasn't until about half an hour later, after I took care of Red once again that I realized something.

He'd stormed off.

He'd slammed the door.

But he hadn't locked it.

This might be my only chance to escape.

Chapter Nine

Ace

"Why isn't she snapping out of it?" Aram asked. "She's looking better."

On the outside, yeah, she was.

The swelling was going down on her face. The wounds the stitches were holding together were less angry-looking.

She was healing.

But only on the outside.

I'd been operating under the misconception that only humans had issues with their heads. It seemed like something that came with the pesky shit like a conscience and a soul. Anxiety, depression, and psychosis issues were nonexistent in our world. At least as far as I could tell.

So watching Red seem to suffer with it was frustrating for many reasons.

First, because we needed to know who'd done it, so we could pay it back.

Second, because I didn't know the protocol for a psychotic or traumatized fucking demon. What were the possible repercussions of that? It wasn't like there would ever be an end to that torment if I couldn't figure it out and fix it.

"I'm looking into it," I assured Aram, trying not to sound as frustrated as I was by his running monologue about Red's condition.

We were all fucking worried.

We didn't need to be constantly reminded.

"What is the nurse saying?" Drex asked, swirling his glass, but not drinking.

"Not much of anything," I mumbled, getting up to scan the spines of the books in the library, trying to see if there was an old text I'd forgotten about that might hold the answers we all had. "What?" I snapped when I felt their gazes on me.

"Just wondering if you were being your usual charming self is all, boss man," Daemon said, shooting me that cocky smirk of his.

"He's got a point," Drex agreed, nodding. "I mean, you did stick her with ketamine. Twice."

"Did you geniuses have another way to get her across the country without raising alarm bells with the humans?" I asked, turning to face them. "It's not my job to be nice to her. Someone else wants to charm information out of her, you're welcome to."

"Charm, he must be talking about me," Daemon decided, getting an eye-roll from Bael, but none of us moved to stop him, knowing that he was likely the only one of us who could get anywhere with her. Especially after I fucked with her head and body, confusing her, making her hate me.

Deamon, in his short time on the human plane, had proven time and time again that he had a way with the human women. The shit that didn't work on the women of our kind was like catnip to the ones here.

"Daemon," I called, hating myself already, but not being able to stop the words from coming out either.

"Yeah, boss?"

"Don't fuck her," I told him, getting a brow raise.

"I have other charms," he said, shrugging. If he was reading into my warning, he didn't let on.

I knew better than to hope the others would show me the same respect.

"We don't fuck hostages," I clarified before they could read too much into it.

"Except for Ly," Drex clarified.

"Watch it," I snapped, sighing.

"This place is a morgue," Drex declared, throwing back his drink, then moving to stand. "I'm going to the club."

"Is this really the time for that?" Aram asked, annoyed. "Red is—"

"Practically catatonic? Yeah, noticed that," Drex said. "You know I give a shit about Red, but her life being on hold doesn't mean mine needs to be," he told Aram, then made his way out the door.

"What?" I snapped, looking at Bael who was giving me a look.

To that, he shrugged. "Not my business."

"I'm telling you to make it your business," I demanded.

While he was never outwardly defiant or disrespectful, Bael's tendency toward seeing himself as separate from the rest of us—despite being in the same boat—made him difficult to deal with on good days. And there weren't many of those with him.

"He's spent every spare minute at that club for months."

I didn't keep tabs on all of them. I was their leader, not their fucking father. I didn't ask where they were going when they left or demand to know the details of their private lives.

I knew Drex was gone a lot. But seeing as there wasn't much to do around the house unless we were partying, I figured he was looking for a way to entertain himself. As was his right. I'd long since stopped finding society interesting, choosing instead to stay in, to read, to keep on top of trends so we never came off as "out of time" while the world moved forward around us.

I didn't realize he spent all his time at one place.

I couldn't imagine why the fuck it mattered.

"And?" I asked, shrugging.

"Do you know what club he's going to?" Bael asked.

I had to admit, he might have been a dick, but he'd been quick to pick up on generations full of knowledge I'd thrown at him, learning how to use appliances, new lingo, how human society worked. It was impressive.

The fact that he knew the differences between clubs at all was far further than the rest of us would have been had we just appeared in this much more modern era.

"Clearly, I don't. I can't imagine it matters."

"He's at Sanctuary," Bael supplied, the name meaning nothing to me.

"It's a kink club," Seven explained.

"Who the fuck cares?" I asked. Drex's proclivity toward punishment styles of sex was well known, had been for years. Luckily, human women had been enjoying getting their asses smacked and air supply cut off since the beginning of time.

"For people like us," Seven explained.

"We're not people."

"Exactly," Bael piped in.

"Are you telling me there is a demon club around here and this is the first I'm fucking hearing about it?"

"It's not just us," Seven said. "There's not that many of us stuck here. And not many in this area of the world. But there are others who shouldn't exist, like us, there."

"When have I ever been someone for subtleties?" I asked.

"There are shifters, Children of Lilith, and blood-suckers and all sorts of shit," Seven informed me, words landing like a bomb.

Shifters, whatever.

We'd been clashing with various shifters for as long as I could remember.

But incubi, succubi, and fucking vampires? In the area? All in one club? That was something I should have known about ages ago. Especially if Drex was spending time around all of them.

"It's called Sanctuary for a reason," Seven explained. "The owner managed to get some witches to spell the place. No one can fight there. Everyone is just there for a good time."

Just because no one could fight while there didn't mean enemies couldn't be made.

And while shifters and Children of Lilith could be killed if necessary, the same couldn't be said about the blood-suckers. Issues with them could last a hundred years or more.

"I need to know why no one thought it was important to tell me that—"

"Ay, yo, boss man," Daemon called, coming down the stairs, hands up. "Don't shoot the messenger here, but the pretty nurse isn't in the room."

"She's probably in the bathroom," I told him. "She's been taking baths." And my pathetic ass had been listening to her run them every day, refusing to let my hand reach down and deal with the aching hard-on just the idea of her in a bath gave me.

"Afraid not," Daemon said, shrugging. "The door was unlocked."

I'd stormed out.

I remembered slamming the door.

But not locking it.

"*Fuck*," I hissed, turning, rushing out of the room.

"Spread out," Bael demanded, taking charge even though he was one of the lowest men on the totem pole.

They would check out the house.

She wasn't going to be in the house.

If she saw a way out, she was going to take it. Especially with how I'd been treating her.

She was on the run.

In the middle of winter.

Running blind, not even knowing what state she was in, let alone how far we were from anyone who would help her.

Grabbing my coat, I flew out the front door, feeling the bite of the air as soon as I crossed onto the front step.

Objectively, I found eighty degrees chilly, but this was different. This was a deep winter night that was slipping below zero. Add in the wind chill as it whipped around, and it wasn't looking good for her out there alone, likely lost.

Even if she'd layered on Red's wardrobe and brought a blanket, she wasn't going to be able to keep herself warm for long.

Succumbing to the elements was surprisingly easy for the humans considering they'd adapted to damn near every climate on Earth for thousands of years.

I hadn't ever experienced it myself, but I recognized the sensations as they assaulted my system. I'd read about them thousands of times.

My heart hammered. My throat felt tight. My thoughts raced and crashed into one another.

"Josephine!" I yelled, barely able to hear it myself over the whipping of the wind.

She wouldn't go into the woods. Horror movies made women seem a lot dumber than any of them I'd ever known.

The woods were dark and dangerous, from falling down a cliff, falling in a river, or being attacked by a predator.

A smart woman would look for a road.

And Josephine was a smart woman.

Decision made, I ran in that direction, eyes peeled to the trees lining it, figuring she would want to stay somewhat hidden, but close enough to the street that she could rush out into it if she saw a car coming.

Not knowing, of course, that cars didn't come this way. Because our property stretched far and wide.

But I ran to the end of said property and back.

And nothing.

She wasn't there.

Or, at least, she wasn't close enough to the road for me to see.

The panic rose, a tight grip on my system, holding me at a knife's edge of my control.

"Josephine!" I yelled, feeling the last bit of it snap.

There was no stopping it.

My tongue forked. My fingertips elongated. The pressure at my temples suggested my horns were starting to poke through.

It had been a long time since I lost control.

Since Lenore had wandered off and gotten taken by the shifters.

The difference was, Lenore had been a vital part of my plan to get us back to hell.

Josephine wasn't.

Her disappearance shouldn't have mattered at all, let alone triggered me to lose my shit.

Hopelessness building, I threw myself deeper into the forest that lined the road, running a useless zigzag pattern, ending up retracing my steps several times over.

And still nothing.

I was about to turn around and head back to the house when the wind picked up again, and I smelled her on the breeze.

It was a combination of the soap Red kept in her shower, the strawberry shampoo in her hair, and just... her. Something sweet and earthy at the same time.

And judging by the direction the wind was blowing, she hadn't made it out to the road yet.

I backtracked toward the house, cutting into the woods near the side.

She wasn't far in.

She'd likely been gone only minutes before Daemon discovered she was gone, had heard me calling her, and moved inward as she saw me take toward the road.

I found her crouched down behind an old stack of firewood from back when we used such things. She wasn't prepared for the weather. She's layered a few of Red's clothing items on, but none of it was enough to keep her warm. Neither was the blanket she had wrapped around her.

Her body racked violently with her shivers. Even in the meager moonlight, I could see her too-pale skin, the tinge of blue to her lips, the bright red tip of her nose.

"Fuck," I hissed, rushing forward, dropping down in front of her, wrapping my arms around her to share the warmth of my coat.

A low, tortured whimper escaped her as her face nuzzled into my neck.

"Don't hurt me," she whined, her arms slipping reluctantly around me under my coat.

"I'm not going to hurt you."

"I told you I wasn't going to be a good captive."

"Yes," I agreed, reaching down to grab her under her ass, hauling her up. "You did," I said, yanking her up. "But you don't need to kill yourself to prove it," I told her, wrapping the edges of my coat as far around her as I could, then lifting her up, starting back toward the house.

"Is she okay?" Lenore asked, rushing to follow behind me as I made my way up the stairs.

"She's cold."

"I will have Ly warm up my rice packs," she told me, calling down for him to do so. "You need to warm from the center," she added.

"I thought you were supposed to chafe the arms and legs," I said, having seen it done for the homeless many times in the past.

"No," Lenore and Josephine said in unison.

"It stresses the heart," Josephine added.

"Get her into something warmer," Lenore demanded. "I will get more blankets."

I moved in front of Red's door before suddenly deciding to take her to my room.

Because I had warmer clothes.

That was the only reason.

"Here. Sit," I demanded, putting her on the bed, yanking the covers up over her as she shivered. "Don't fight me on this," I demanded when I came back from grabbing sweat clothes from the closet. I pulled back the blanket, yanked her up, then reached to pull off her shirt. "I'm not trying to stare at your tits, Josephine," I told her, frustration seeping into my words. "I'm trying to keep you alive," I added, getting a grudging sigh from her, but she let me take off her too-thin shirts, and slip on my warmest hooded sweatshirt.

The bottoms of her pants were wet from likely stepping in the small stream that wrapped around two sides of the property.

She didn't bother to fight me when I yanked them off, and one look at her made me more concerned than relieved that she wasn't making a fuss.

Her eyes seemed a little unfocused. Her breathing was weaker.

"Shit," I hissed, pulling the pants into place, slipping on the socks, then pulling the blankets up over her, trying to seal in whatever warmth I could.

"Get in with her," Lenore said, making me turn to find her coming closer with her heated rice bags, slipping them under Josephine's clothes—one on the chest, one near her groin.

"What?" I asked, shaking my head.

To that, Lenore let out a small, humorless laugh.

"I think you all forget it because you feel cold all the time, but you are all really warm. Hot even. It's like being close to a furnace. Get in there with her. You will warm her up faster than my little heat packs or the blankets alone. I will go make her something warm and sweet to drink."

I didn't bother to ask her why it should be sweet. I didn't think the coven of witches she came from got much right in the world, but it was hard to argue with them knowing more about how to recover from exposure to the elements than I did.

So I took a steadying breath, moving to the other side of the bed, pulling off my shirt and pants, then climbing in.

I thought it would be difficult, what with being naked around the woman who had been problematic for my sex drive. But the touch of her frigid skin as I pulled her over my body was enough to chase away anything but what I recognized as concern for her, maybe even fear that she wasn't going to make it.

Humans were so fragile that way.

Five extra minutes too long in the cold, and it could all be over.

I tried to convince myself that I gave a shit because it would be inconvenient to have to find a new nurse to help with Red. Though, I knew it wasn't that. But since I wasn't ready to unravel that, I went ahead and forced the thoughts from my mind.

It took a solid forty-five minutes before she stopped shivering. And there was one heart-stopping moment where I waited for her to take her next breath.

It was maybe another twenty minutes after that when I felt her take one slow, deep breath, exhaling it.

"For someone who acts like he's always half-frozen to death, you are really warm," she mumbled, turning her head so her colder cheek pressed to my chest. "You ever hear that old saying about people that have cold hands have warm hearts?" she mused, sounding half-asleep.

"The only thing warm about me is my skin, Josephine."

"That's mostly true," she agreed, her hand pressing flat against my pectoral muscle, and it was becoming harder and harder to remember I was here just to warm her up. And easier and easier to notice just how fucking naked I was.

"It's completely true. Don't think just because I saved you tonight that I'm a decent man. I'm not."

"You love Red."

"I'm responsible for Red," I clarified.

"Someone who feels responsible for someone gets them the medical care they clearly need. They don't sit up with them every night reading them poetry."

"Don't read into things that don't mean anything."

"Don't be so hard on yourself," she shot back. "It must be difficult to be a biker, ah, leader..."

"President," I clarified, getting a snort out of her.

"Okay. *President.* That's an obnoxious title, but okay. I get it is hard to be that, to have all of them looking to you for leadership. But it doesn't mean you have to be a complete dick."

"I was this way before I became their president," I told her.

"Rough upbringing?" she asked, her fingers gliding over my shoulder, my upper arm.

"Something like that."

Not many men lived the life I had lived before Earth and came out of it kind and well-adjusted. I don't know what the fuck happened with Daemon. In that case, I figured his brother just got the lion's share of the seriousness in that family. Or that Daemon himself shirked most of his responsibilities in the underworld, leaving Bael to pick up the slack, and Daemon to fuck around and have fun.

"You?" I asked, not even believing it was coming out of my mouth as it was. I didn't ask fucking humans personal questions. I didn't care enough about any of them to get to know them. And yet here I was, asking a woman I would need to execute in a few weeks what her fucking childhood was like. What was wrong with me?

"Not as hard as a lot of other people, no."

"You don't judge your hardships on the fact that other people have it worse."

"It wasn't awful. We were just really poor. And then my mom passed."

"What about your father?"

"He wasn't in the picture after he knocked up a coworker."

"So you have no one."

I wanted to believe I wanted to learn this information so that I knew if people would be looking for her or not once she was dead. She was relatively young, very pretty, a nurse. That was the kind of woman who made the news cycle nonstop when she was missing or murdered.

"Not anymore," she admitted, wiggling a bit, and it was becoming problematic. "I had someone. But that ended before I moved to Utah. It's just me. I guess you picked the ideal victim, huh?" she asked, sighing out her breath. "No one even to look for me."

I wanted to tell her not to call herself a victim.

But that was exactly what I'd made her.

I wanted to tell her not to feel so sorry for herself.

But what right did I have to say that, when I was putting her in this situation?

"You have coworkers who will have noticed you are missing by now."

"They don't like me."

"Now you sound like you're pitying yourself."

"Hey," she snapped, planting her hands on either side of my body, pushing up to look down at me. "You don't know the situation, so you don't get to tell me I am pitying myself."

"What's not to like about you?" I asked.

"I'm new. That's usually enough reason sometimes."

"For insecure people, yes," I agreed. "Sounds like you should pity them instead of yourself. Imagine how miserable they must be to dislike you just because you're new."

"I guess," she agreed, reaching up to tuck her hair behind her ear, letting out a growling noise when it slipped right back out again. "This stupid hair," she added, sighing, as she rolled off to my side, but didn't put much space between us.

"What's wrong with your hair?"

"I cut it," she told me, shaking her head at herself. "It used to be long and I cut most of it off. That was actually what I was thinking about when you..."

"Abducted you," I supplied when she didn't want to say the words.

"How can you say it so easily?" she asked, brows knitting. "Like it's nothing? It's a big deal to kidnap someone. Even to bikers."

"I've told you, and shown you through example time and time again, that I am not a good man, Josephine. I won't apologize for it. It's how we have all survived this long."

"Just barely though, right?" she asked, looking over toward where Red's room was. "Maybe if you tried to be better men, you would be able to take her to a hospital for proper treatment instead of snatching people off of the streets."

"Near-death experiences make you mouthy," I observed, getting a strange choking laugh sound out of her.

"Near-death experiences make me realize you must find me valuable enough not to kill, so I figure I can get away with a lot more than I have so far," she told me, climbing out of the bed, grabbing frantically at the waist of my pants when they immediately started to fall down when she stood.

"Where do you think you're going?"

"Down to the... what the hell?" she asked, reaching into her pants, pulling out the rice bag I'd forgotten all about.

"Heated rice pack," I explained.

"For like... cramps?" she asked, testing the weight of it in her hands.

"And warming up hypothermic women who don't realize how fragile they are."

"I'm not fragile," she snapped, lowering her eyes at me.

Right.

We were in the evolution of womanhood where words like that no longer made them feel cherished, but condescended to. As much as I researched the changes in the world, the social ones were the hardest for me to wrap my head around.

Where I came from, everyone had been equal since the beginning of time. This shit with the humans since the beginning of time, hating on one another for race or sex or orientation, it was absurd. But it kept us busy down in hell, so we couldn't bitch too much.

"In terms of how easily your life could end, yes you are. No more fragile than the average man in that respect, but still fragile. What?" I asked when her brows scrunched together, her lips pursed.

"Sometimes you say things in a really strange way," she said, shaking her head. "Like you're not from here or from this time or something. Maybe it's because you read so much," she decided. "My mom used to accidentally adopt a southern accent if she watched too many movies based there."

That was the perk of more modern humans, I guessed. They were more far removed from the 'myths' and 'lore' of old. When they encountered something that didn't fit in with their world, they found easier explanations that didn't involve the supernatural, heaven, or hell.

It made it easier to exist among them. Easier than when having a birthmark in the wrong place could end up with you being dragged through the streets and hanged.

Red always took an immense amount of pleasure in the fact that she was found guilty of witchcraft three times during the Burning Times. Luckily for us, we'd always managed to get her out before they tied her to a stake, lit her up, and realized she couldn't die.

Remember that time they caught me rolling around with the priest? she would bring up randomly through the years. *And since a priest couldn't possibly get horny, I must have spelled him into it. Humans were a lot of fun when they were so dumb.*

Only Red would consider witch trials—both the inquisition sort and the physical tests—fun.

That was why it was so hard to watch her waste away. She'd always been so full of life, someone who managed to take every shitty hand she was dealt and make a win come out of it.

"Yeah," I agreed, snapping out of my swirling thoughts. "That must be it."

"How old *are* you?" she asked.

"Ancient," I answered honestly, but got a snort out of her.

"You look like you're in your mid-thirties."

I did.

As I had for hundreds of years.

"How old are you?" I asked instead of confirming or denying her assumption.

"Twenty-seven."

Twenty-seven.

Twenty-seven years passed in a blink for us. But it was enough time for her to be conceived, born, to go through all those formative years, go to college, lose everyone who ever meant anything to her, then find herself abducted and held captive.

She wasn't going to make it to twenty-eight.

That thought shouldn't have bothered me.

But I couldn't shake the dark mood it made course through me.

"What?" she asked, shifting feet.

"Nothing."

"You look angry."

"That's my face," I told her, feeling my lips twitch despite myself when she let out a small laugh. Light, girlish. It wasn't a sound many women shared with me. I liked it more than I had a right to.

"Do you ever smile?"

"I don't remember the last time I had reason to. No," I said when her face went sad. "Don't feel bad for me," I demanded. I had never been plagued with something resembling a conscience, but I couldn't take pity from a woman whose life I was going to need to take eventually.

"I—" she started, trailing off then I threw off the covers and climbed naked out of the bed.

Nudity tended to work well in ending uncomfortable conversations.

Sometimes, because of desire.

Other times, because of shock.

I didn't let myself stop to see which one Josephine had on her face, just walked to my bathroom for a shower.

Of the cold variety.

Chapter Ten

I almost died.

Legitimately.

I wasn't exaggerating.

I'd been stupid and reckless and a little too optimistic about how close the house was to a main road or another house, anywhere that I could find help.

When I'd heard Ace coming, I'd panicked, gotten all turned around, then somehow found myself closer to the house again.

Crouching there by that pile of wood, I had all the classic signs of hypothermia. The shivering, the slow pulse, the shallow breathing, the drowsiness, and even confusion.

The confusion maybe most of all.

Since I had been sure in those moments that Ace's eyes had been glowing red, that his tongue had been forked, that there had been weird bone-line things starting to jut out of his forehead.

Clearly, my consciousness and my unconsciousness had merged, creating some weird, otherworldly creature out of the man kneeling before me, my captor that was there to save me.

I didn't remember much of anything after that until I woke up feeling like a furnace was underneath and around me.

It took a long couple of minutes before I realized that the warmth was coming from a body. More specifically, Ace's body.

I should have jumped off of him, ran away screaming.

I didn't do that, though.

And I tried to convince myself that I stayed because I was cold, because it was important to warm up completely after a brush with hypothermia like that.

I knew the truth, though.

I didn't want to move because it felt good being close to him. And not just because he was warm.

Was that screwed up?

Yes. Yes, absolutely.

I had almost just *died*.

Because I was trying to run away from him.

Then there I was, snuggling up to him, making small talk with him, and enjoying it more than it could have possibly been healthy psychologically.

Then, oh, then, he had to get out of that bed.

Naked.

The man just stood up and bared it all.

Let's just say... there was a lot to be bared.

I was annoyed at myself for noticing, but he'd surprised me. I hadn't been able to look away fast enough.

Yeah, that was the story I was going with.

I never really considered what Ace was like under all those hoodies and grandpa sweaters.

Apparently, he was built much like a Greek god was. He was nearly six-and-a-half feet of sculpted, yet not bulky, muscle. I guess I pictured him always curled up with a book, not working out. But, clearly, he had a dedicated regimen for his body to look that good. From his eight—yes, eight—pack and right on down to those deep dips of his Adonis muscles.

Normally, that was as far as the average woman could see of the above-average man.

But when my eyes followed those indents, they didn't meet the waistband of his pants. Oh, no.

They found more skin.

Ace was big *every*where.

And he was even bigger still because he was hard.

There had been a deep, undeniable pulsating need inside when my eyes landed on his cock. That primal, cavewoman part of me could practically feel the fullness of him inside.

The sensation was so intense that even after he turned to walk away—and we weren't even going to talk about that biteable ass of his—I'd needed to press my thighs together for one long minute to calm the chaos there before I could even focus enough to walk out of his room.

"Hey there, pretty lady," a voice said as soon as I moved into the hall.

I turned to find who had to be Daemon, even though he hadn't visited with Red. From what I understood, Daemon and Bael were new additions to the team or gang or club, whatever it was that they called themselves. I figured maybe they didn't check on her because they didn't know her like everyone else.

Daemon looked younger than the others, but with the same rough-and-tumble biker look that most of them had with his dark hair, tattoos, and several visible piercings.

"I, ah, hey."

"Where's the boss man?"

"Taking a shower," I told him, shrugging.

"Does he know you're out here in the hall?"

"He didn't tell me to stay put," I said, getting a smirk from Daemon.

"I like the way your mind works," he decided, moving forward, draping an arm around my shoulders. "How about I tag along while you break some more rules? Want to dig around in the basement? Deface some of the fine art? Rip some random pages out of pivotal books in Ace's library?"

I understood that while he was being playful about it, and giving me the illusion of freedom, that Daemon was just a different kind of prison guard.

"I would like to raid the kitchen, actually," I admitted.

I'd been served exactly two kinds of meals in my time with these people.

When Lenore fed me, it was very much the "twigs and leaves" variety of food. She was, I had been informed, vegetarian.

When Minos was the one feeding me, it was usually uncooked pieces of random vegetables like celery or zucchini along with a slab of some sort of meat that was cooked without any sort of seasoning. And "cooked" was being generous about how rare the meat was.

I hadn't eaten a carbohydrate in what felt like ages.

"Then to the kitchen we shall go," Daemon declared grandly, leading me down the stairs and into the massive kitchen.

"Lenore?" I asked, waving toward the oversized windows where dozens of herbs and flowers were lined up.

"She had a massive outdoor garden in the summer. She has some things growing now too. In, ah, cold frames or something like that. Ly is building her a greenhouse."

"Can I?" I asked, waving toward the fridge.

"Help yourself, princess," he invited, hopping himself up on the counter, reaching for a mug of coffee there.

I could feel his gaze on me as I went through the fridge, finding some vegetables that I could cook, then rummaging around the pantry to find some questionably old pasta to make with it.

I'd just dropped the shells into the boiling water when Ace's roar seemed to sound loud enough to make the walls shake.

"Uh oh. Daddy's mad," Daemon said, a wicked smile pulling at his lips when he looked at me.

"Damn it," Ace roared, tearing down the stairs, almost falling forward with his momentum when his gaze fell on me and he tried to stop quickly. "What the fuck?" he asked, looking between the two of us.

"The pretty lady was hungry. I showed her the kitchen."

"I didn't say she could leave the room," Ace snapped, giving Daemon a hard look.

"You also didn't lock the door," Daemon shot back, surprising me with the challenge in his tone.

It didn't escape Ace, either, whose eyes went harder than usual as he looked at the younger man.

"Why don't you go change the oil on the bikes," Ace suggested, a clear punishment for the younger man's attitude to someone who was supposed to be his boss.

"It's freezing out there, man," Daemon complained, taking a sip of his coffee.

"Yeah, that's not going to be enjoyable," Ace agreed, chin lifting. "You're still going to do it."

To that, Daemon sighed and jumped off the counter. "Maybe we will have some more adventures together in the future, pretty lady," he said, then grabbed a coat off a hook by the door, and moved outside.

"Did he really do anything wrong?" I asked, stirring the pasta.

"Are you really questioning how I run my club?"

"Yes, I am," I said, smiling. "He was clearly trying to keep an eye on me until you became less... indisposed."

"He's a headstrong little shit," Ace said, making his way to the coffee machine.

"Well, yeah," I agreed. "But he's harmless."

"None of us are harmless, Josephine. The sooner you learn that, the better," he said, reaching into the cabinet to grab a mug, holding one up to me, a question in his eyes.

"Yes, thank you. But do you have sugar?" I knew from the fridge that milk wasn't an option.

"Yeah. What are you making?"

"Well, your pantry and fridge are woefully empty," I informed him. "But I found some ancient pasta, some tomatoes, and spinach. Do you think Lenore would mind if I stole some herbs? This will barely be edible without some."

"Take whatever you want."

"That's not what I asked," I told him, shaking my head.

"It's fine."

"Again, that's not what I asked."

"Lenore is the only one of us who might be considered generous," Ace clarified. "She won't mind sharing. She comes from a society that shared everything."

"Oh, that must have been nice."

"It's antiquated and backward."

"Why are you so cynical about everything? Just because something isn't for you doesn't mean it isn't for someone else."

At that, his lips twitched ever so slightly at one side. The beginnings of a smile. Miracles would never cease, it seemed.

"Give you a little freedom, and you get an attitude on you," he mused, tone close to playful.

"See, your mistake is thinking I didn't have an attitude all along," I said, shrugging. "I was just scared and then drugged and then in isolation from everyone, so you didn't experience it fully. But I figure if you saved me from the elements, I am on pretty safe footing here now. You can expect more attitude from now on. I think someone needs to put you in your place once in a while," I added, shooting him a smirk.

The surprisingly warm look in his eyes suggested he might not mind it, either.

"Come on," he said a while later. After I'd cooked, eaten, and left my mess for Daemon on Ace's orders because 'he could use something to do other than eating pussy every minute of the day.'

"Back to banishment," I declared, feeling a little happier with a stomach full of pasta and two cups of coffee.

"No one has checked on Red in hours," he reminded me, making me feel guilty. True, she seemed as stable as she was going to get, but she still needed to be cared for.

"I think she is going to need someone," I said as I followed Ace up the stairs. "For, you know, whatever is going on inside her. I don't understand why she is still so out of it," I admitted as Ace opened the door, leading me inside.

"Don't think it will come to that," he told me, moving to his usual chair, picking up the poetry book off the nightstand.

"Do you really think Red likes poetry?" I asked, checking her for a fever, then looking over her wounds. She was healing, slowly but surely. In another week or so, I would likely be able to take out most of the stitches.

I wasn't sure what was going to happen to me after that, though. It was a thought that made sleep difficult some nights. If I stopped being useful, what would they want with me? I mean, I knew their names. I knew their faces. But I also had no idea where we even were. If they just drove me to another state or something and dropped me off, I wouldn't have nearly enough information to provide to the police to get them involved.

"Probably not," Ace said, snorting. "She would be sitting here rolling her eyes at me."

"Then why would you read it to her?" I asked.

"Because I can't read the shit she reads."

"What does she read?" I asked, watching as he gestured to the nightstand.

Curious, I reached inside, shuffling some papers around, several of which with the same name written on them.

Marceaus.

"Mar-see-us," I read, sounding it out. "Who is that?"

"Mar-kay-us," Ace corrected. "He's someone important to Red."

"Does he know what happened to her? Why isn't he here?" I asked, offended for her. It was us women against the shitty men who didn't appreciate us. I might not have known Red, but I was going to go ahead and be angry for her.

"She hasn't seen him in a long time," Ace told me, shrugging.

She was still clearly hung up on him, though.

My heart ached for her as I went into the second drawer, finding the book Ace was making me look for.

"*Denver*," I said, reading the title. The cover didn't give much away. "What is it about?"

"A woman who has an affair with a man she calls Denver because she doesn't know his real name."

"It's a romance," I said.

"It's a sex book," he scoffed.

"How do you know that if you haven't read it?" I shot back, rolling my eyes.

My mother had been a hardcore romance reader. We used to spend a lot of weekends at the library since it was one of the few places you could go and not have to spend any money. I would head to the kid section and grab books about fairies and wizards and trolls. My mom would go to the adult section and clear half a shelf of romances every week. She used to tell me that they were more than love books, that it got a bad rep, that I should never, ever judge someone by what kinds of books they liked to read because I didn't know what they were going through in life, and what kinds of stories helped them escape from it for a while.

I'd been a hardcore romance book defender in her honor, even if I hadn't ever had the kind of free time that allowed me to read much. If I did, I was pretty sure I would pick up her favorite genre as a tribute to her.

"You want me to give it a chance?" he asked, brow raised.

"Yes. Is that too much to ask?"

To that, he shrugged, holding out his hand so I could press the book into it.

"Fine," he agreed, flipping open to the bookmarked page of the well-loved book as I turned to make my way back toward the couch.

His voice filled the room, stopping me dead in my tracks with his words.

This time, not because they were calm and soothing.

Oh, no.

"With my ass fully plugged, Denver bent me over the desk in the office, admiring his handiwork, the bright

red handprints that had to have been marring the pale white skin of my cheeks. I tried to turn my head to look at him, to see his black eyes, the way his jaw got tight when he was imagining fucking me, like I had seen so many times before. But his hand slammed down on the back of my neck, holding me in place. A long, tense moment passed of him just staring at me before, suddenly, his finger flicked the hot pink plug buried deep in my ass, sending an unexpected surge of desire through my system, making my pussy even wetter than it already was, something I didn't even think was possible.

'Tell me you want my cock buried in your wet cunt, Eva,' he demanded, making my hips buck up toward him in silent invitation as his hand moved from the back of my neck to slip into my hair, sliding down the strands until he was halfway down, knowing it hurt more there, knowing how much I liked that. Then yanking hard enough to make me arch as far as my body would allow.

Denver didn't like to be kept waiting.

Or to be disobeyed.

Or even to give me his real goddamn name.

But I didn't need to know his name to know I wanted his giant cock stretching me as I was helpless to do anything but take it, but beg for release from the relentless ache of desire.

'I want your cock buried in me,' I told him, hearing the rawness of need in my voice.

'That's not what I said,' he scolded.

I knew it was coming a second before the belt snapped across the lowest part of my ass, the bite of it stinging against my pussy at the same time, the pain—and the pleasure it brought me—so intense that I nearly came right then and there.

A part of me wanted to pretend like I didn't know what he wanted me to say, to get more of that sharp, perfect pain I loved so much, the pain that no other man had ever given me, the pain that only Denver knew I enjoyed so much.

The other part of me, though, needed to feel him inside me. And if I kept testing him, he wouldn't fuck me as punishment. He would whip my ass, then push me down on the bed and fuck my mouth instead."

I turned back at Ace's sudden silence, finding his gaze on me, his head cocked to the side, reading my face as soon as he could see it.

"Not a sex book?" he asked, voice as rough as my nerve endings felt.

"I, ah," I started, needing to stop to clear my throat. "I'm sure there is a plot somewhere," I insisted.

"Hm," he said, flipping randomly to another page.

"'We can't do this here,' I insisted as Denver's fingers slipped inside my panties, pushing inside me, and thrusting hard and fast.

I could hear the conversation of a couple walking down the street, commenting on the decor in the window of the store we were currently down the side alley of.

'It looks like we already are,' he corrected, lowering down up under my skirt, licking up my cleft, sealing his lips around my clit..."

"Okay," I said, swallowing hard. "It's a sex book," I agreed, feeling the pulsating sensation between my thighs.

"What's the matter?" he asked, rising from his chair, stalking over toward me. "Having trouble hearing?" he asked, opening up the book again like he planned to keep reading.

"Don't," I demanded, feeling like there was a heavy weight pressing on my chest, making breathing hard.

"Why not?" he asked, towering over me. Close. Way, way too close. I would swear his nearness was making the air thicker, harder to breathe in.

"Just don't," I demanded, voice small, airless.

"Having flashbacks?" he asked, lips curving up slightly. "To me on my knees, sucking on your clit?" he asked.

God, that felt like forever ago. And yet only yesterday somehow at the same time.

"Ace, please," I demanded, my resolve to dislike him disintegrating with each passing second.

"Please what?" he asked, taking one more step forward, sucking up what was left of the air away from me as I craned my neck up to keep eye-contact. "Please walk away right now? Or please eat you out until you lose your voice?" he asked, and I swear I could feel him between my thighs with just his words.

"We can't," I objected, proud I could force any rational thoughts to form when my head felt slow and foggy.

"We can," he corrected.

"I... I think I have Stockholm Syndrome," I admitted out loud.

"Do you feel grateful toward me?" he asked.

"God, no," I admitted, getting a small chuckle out of him, a sound so rare that I found it fascinating.

"Do you admire me or agree with my plans?"

"No."

"Do you care about my needs or happiness?"

"Ah, not particularly," I said, feeling like he was talking me into a trap, but not sure how to free myself.

"Do you think that sleeping with me will help save you, or gain you something?"

"No."

"Then maybe it isn't Stockholm Syndrome. Maybe you just want to fuck me."

He made it sound so rational, so easy.

I couldn't tell anymore what was logical and what wasn't. What was fact, and what was a manipulation of the truth.

All I knew was he was right.

The heaviness in my chest, the weight on my lower stomach, my shallow breathing, the ache between my thighs, it all spoke to one thing.

I wanted to sleep with him.

Captor or not.

Weird psychological survival mechanism or not.

My body wanted his right then.

And I was having a hard time thinking of any reasons to deny it any longer.

"Josephine," he called, making me look up, finding him watching me with those strange red-flecked eyes. "If it's no, it's no. I don't want it if you have to talk yourself into it," he told me, shrugging.

"It's wrong," I told him, my hand lifting, fingertip running up his chest.

"Most likely," he agreed, nodding.

"It's a bad idea," I went on as my hand went to the side of his neck.

"Almost certainly," he agreed, clearly having his own internal struggles with the idea of it happening, but too far gone to care.

Judging by the way my skin seemed to hum when I pressed my body close to his, I was at that point as well.

Too far gone to care.

It was probably wrong.

It was definitely a bad idea.

But I wanted it. He wanted it.

There would be time for a proper psychological analysis and therapy down the road.

Right now, this was going to happen.

Chapter Eleven

Jo

I should have been nervous.

Sex with a new person always had that effect, and it should have been more amplified with him seeing as he was my damn captor and all.

But all I could seem to feel as his hand grabbed the back of my neck, and his lips crashed down on mine for the first time, was a bone-deep kind of rightness, like everything in me was responding to him.

He kissed like I expected for a man like him. Hard, deep, almost bruising with his intensity, but thoroughly, focusing on that one thing for what felt like hours, until my lips felt swollen and tingly, until every inch of skin felt heated and over-sensitive.

His fingers slid upward, sifting into my hair, curling, and pulling hard, making my head jerk back as a surprised gasp escaped me. Leaning down, he ran his lips down the side of my neck, teasing his tongue over my pulse point when he found it.

His hands moved, grabbing me at the waist as he turned, pulling me down on his lap as he dropped onto the couch, giving him better access as his fingers snagged the hem of my shirt, dragging it upward.

As soon as my head was free, though, he stopped, yanking it back down, trapping my arms at my sides as he leaned forward and sucked my nipple into his mouth. A jolt of need shot through me, a white-hot spark that moved down my spine to settle between my legs, making my hips wiggle against his lap, needing the movement, the friction.

A low, growling noise rumbled through Ace as his teeth nipped for a second before he moved across my chest, continuing the same torment there. Until my nipples were hard and aching, until my breasts felt heavy, until a flush had broken out across my chest, making me feel warm all over.

His hands grabbed my hips again, yanking me up off his lap, so he could slide my pants down over my ass, helping me out of the legs.

But just as I was going to settle back on his lap, his hands sank into my ass, yanking up so hard and fast that I couldn't do anything but gasp and flail out my arms as he practically tossed me up on the back cushions of the couch, leveling my sex right over his face.

There was a second of mortified uncertainty, feeling like I was going to suffocate the man, making me yank up my hips away from him, trying to figure out how to get back down.

But Ace's hands sank into my ass, yanking me back down, and running his tongue up my cleft, finding my clit, and working it in fast, relentless circles.

Yeah, all thoughts to objections fell away, even as I tried to find a way to brace myself as my thighs started to shake.

With nothing else to do, I leaned into the wall, hands going down to grab the back of the couch as he continued to devour me, driving me up so quickly that I felt like it was hard to find my breath.

One hand slipped from my ass, going between my thighs, thrusting inside, and turning to run over my top wall.

It was seconds, literally only seconds, after that the orgasm slammed through my system, making me cry out as my entire body seemed like it shook with the intensity.

"I can't... I can't," I whimpered as the waves started to ebb, and Ace's tongue started working me again.

"You can," he objected, yanking me back down onto his lap, leaving my clit alone as his fingers fucked me. Harder, faster. "See?" he asked a moment later as my walls started to tighten around him. "There," he added when the pulsations started, slow and deep, then faster and harder as I fell into his chest, crying out against his shoulder. "Told you," he added, sounding smug as I slowly started to come back down.

"Only you could sound so condescending during sex," I grumbled against his neck before shifting upward, catching his strange red-flecked eyes for a moment before sealing my lips over his. But this time I was in control. It was slower, deeper, less demanding, giving my brain a chance to recover from the back-to-back orgasms enough for me to think straight.

My hands slid down his chest, drawing up his shirt, lips slipping from his to pull off his shirt.

I wasn't, as a whole, someone who liked to rush. And after two solid orgasms, I felt a little more level-headed. Enough that I knew I wanted a chance to explore his body, maybe even torment him a little bit.

I took my time, running my fingers over his chest, around his nipples, down into the indents of his abdominal muscles, feeling them tense under my inspection.

Slowly, I slid off his lap, slipping between his thighs on the floor, my hands running from his knees and upward before moving inward, feeling the hard length of him straining against his pants.

A rumbling noise moved through him, a sound that made my sex clench hard, as I drew down the waistband of his pants, freeing him, feeling an aching hollowness between my thighs, needing to remind myself that we would get there, that I didn't want to rush it.

My gaze found and held his as I moved forward, running my tongue over the head of his cock, watching his lips fall open, his breath catch in his chest.

I didn't need any more encouragement than that.

Ducking my head, I slipped him inside my mouth, taking him deep as my hand curled around the base of him, stroking as I sucked, feeling him get harder and bigger still as I worked him.

Ace's hand slammed on the back of my head, fingertips curling into my skull. His hips started to thrust upward as I slipped down, making me take him deeper and deeper.

"Fuck, no," he growled, hips settling, fingers grabbing a clump of my hair and yanking until his cock slid out of my mouth. When I glanced up at him, his eyes looked redder than ever, almost like they were glowing.

His breathing was hard and fast, and I found myself oddly transfixed with the rise and fall of his chest for a moment while he tried to pull himself together.

"Get up here," he demanded, patting his thigh, making need pierce through me as I pushed up, and went to move over him. "What?" he asked when I paused, stiffened.

"Condom," I grumbled, annoyed for there to be any delay in getting him inside me. But also not stupid enough to have unprotected sex with a near-stranger.

A grunt escaped Ace as he grabbed my ass, pulling me tightly against him, then knifed up, getting to his feet, waiting for my legs to wrap around his hips, my arms to encircle his neck. His hands sank in, dragging my cleft along his hard length even as he started moving across the room.

It wasn't until he bent forward that I realized two things.

One, he was going in the nightstand for a condom.

Two, we were still in Red's room.

"Ace," I whined in his ear as he turned to walk back to the couch. "We can't."

"We can," he countered, dragging me against him again, doing that growling noise when I let out a stifled moan.

"Not here," I objected, trying to unwrap my legs.

Again, that growl. I shouldn't have found it as sexy as I did.

Before I understood his intention, he was across the room and opening the door.

"Ace, no!" I hissed, trying to drop down, but his hands were holding me in place as he moved down the hall and into his room.

"There," he said, kicking his bedroom door closed, then making his way toward the bed.

His body pressed mine into the mattress as he slid us up toward the pillows, his lips sealed over mine.

Ace pressed up and back to sit on his heels, and I found myself transfixed by watching him slide on the condom, his gaze on me half the time, hard, hungry.

Finished, his hands gripped my hips, dragging me up onto his lap, dragging my legs up, then slamming inside me without warning.

"Oh my G—" I cried out, sucking in a greedy breath before I could even get the last word out, feeling a pinch at the fullness of him inside me, pulling my hips back slightly to ease the ache. "You're too big," I said, even as I felt my walls adjusting to the invasion.

That grumbling noise moved through Ace again as he lowered my legs, yanking them wide, and reaching between, relentlessly working my clit until an unexpectedly quick orgasm slammed through my system, the sensation even more intense with the fullness of him inside.

"There," he said as the orgasm subsided, his voice rougher than before. "Better?" he asked, barely waiting for my frantic nod before starting to thrust. A little tentatively at first, still giving me a minute to adjust. But as soon as my hips started grinding up against him, he came over me, and thrust harder, faster, as my arms and legs went around him, as the headboard knocked against the wall.

But just as I felt myself getting close, he pulled out of me, grabbing my hips, flipping me over onto my stomach, and yanking my hips back upward toward him as he surged inside me.

My hand shot out, pushing against the headboard he would have slammed me up against as he got harder, faster, even more unrestrained.

His palm slapped down on my ass, the pain somehow intensifying the pleasure as his other hand moved between my thighs, started working my clit as he thrust harder still, making growling noises that made my walls tighten around him, holding on tighter.

"Come, Josephine," he demanded in a voice that was more growl than speech.

His hips thrust.

His finger swiped.

And I just... shattered.

Ace's hand slammed into the back of my head, stuffing my face deeper into the bedsheets, muffling the cries as I came.

The waves were just started to ebb when he slammed deep, letting out a growl that sounded downright primal as he came.

I collapsed forward, sucking in a shaky breath, planting a hand to turn over and share an exhausted, but satisfied smile with Ace.

But when I turned, that smile froze and fell off my face.

Everything within me tensed.

I swear my heartbeat stuttered to a stop, then surged into overdrive.

It hadn't been a hypothermia hallucination.

His eyes had been red.

They had been glowing.

His tongue had been forked.

There had been horns forcing their way out of his forehead.

But, no.

No, that wasn't possible.

They didn't exist.

It was all allegory, right? That was what I had been raised to believe. Demons weren't actual, physical entities, but represented the inherent evil in all of us that we needed to fight.

They weren't living, breathing, flesh-wearing *men*.

Men who you could unwittingly have sex with.

And make them reveal their true form.

Oh, God.

Oh my *God*.

"Josephine..." Ace started, reaching a hand out toward me, making me suddenly aware of his elongated fingers, their pointed nails.

Talons.

Not nails.

Because he wasn't freaking *human*.

I didn't even realize the scream came from me until Ace shocked backward at the sound of it.

"Stop," Ace demanded, trying to reach for me again.

"No!" I shrieked, yanking away from him, throwing myself off the bed.

I didn't even think.

I didn't pause to consider my best move.

I just ran, stark freaking naked, down the hall, back into Red's room, slamming, and locking the door.

I did pause to grab my clothes off the floor before running into the bathroom, locking that door as well, not knowing much, but knowing I want as many closed and locked doors between us as possible.

That was assuming that doors could stop a demon.

Hell, for all I knew, they could materialize out of thin air.

I suddenly wished I had paid a hell of a lot more attention in Sunday School as a kid. At least I would know what I was up against here then.

My heart was hammering against my ribcage, making me genuinely concerned about a heart attack as I yanked my clothes back on, gaze on the door the whole time.

A demon.

He was a *demon*.

And I'd slept with him.

"Josephine," Ace called through the door, voice soft, almost coaxing.

I wasn't going to answer.

What could I say?

What could *he* say?

Would he try to deny it? Make me disbelieve my own two eyes?

God, I wanted to disbelieve my eyes.

Because demons weren't supposed to exist.

Because even if they did, I shouldn't have been able to cross paths with one.

"Oh, God. Oh, God. Oh, God," I whimpered, dropping down on the side of the tub, pressing my head in my hands.

"You're going to have to come out of there eventually," Ace called.

I was pretty sure I would rather starve to death than go out there with him again.

The sex that had felt damn near other-worldly, apparently, was.

But not the good world.

The freaking underworld.

My stomach churned and heaved, driving bile upward.

I barely made it to the toilet in time, retching until there was nothing left inside.

I dragged myself off the floor, blowing my nose, and reaching for the mouth wash, not wanting to look myself in the mirror, but forcing myself too.

There I was.

Familiar, yet not.

There was a hollowness in my eyes I had never seen there before.

On top of that, there was the evidence of what had just transpired between Ace and me. My lips were swollen. There was a beard burn down the side of my neck, over my chest. I couldn't bear to look any further down, or turn around and see the spanking marks on my butt.

I grabbed a washcloth, covering it in soap and water, and scrubbing at my marks, making them all the redder, but feeling like I had to wipe away the traces of him on my flesh.

It was only after I turned the water off that I heard Ace again.

I guess I thought he might have left.

But there was a small thud, something like a hand or a forehead hitting the door, a deep sigh, and then his footsteps as he made his way out of Red's room.

The tension didn't subside. It was a live wire sparking through my system, making me feel uncomfortable in my own skin.

I stood there until my legs ached before I turned to the shower, turning the water on to scorching, then scrubbing every inch of my skin, trying to wash him away.

But it was no use.

He'd been all over me.

He'd been *inside* of me.

I climbed back into my dirty clothes, not wanting to leave the safety of my locked door.

Eventually, exhaustion had me piling all the towels, washcloths, and hand towels into the bathtub, and climbing in, falling into fitful sleep, uncomfortably dominated by dreams about demons. About one demon, in particular.

But they weren't appropriate dreams about hellfire and pitch-black souls.

Oh, no.

They were other dreams.

The kind that left me waking up feeling needy and sick to my stomach over that need.

That sick feeling became incredibly familiar over the next few days. As did the way my mind raced back and forth, trying to accept this new reality.

Heaven.

Hell.

Demons.

Maybe... angels?

I thought until I drove myself half-crazy.

Then I went ahead and kept thinking.

Chapter Twelve

Ace

I couldn't get that look out of my head.

I'd just fucking barely recovered from an orgasm that made me see white. I'd been around for a long time. I'd fucked many women. It always had its appeal, but it hadn't ever been for me like I imagined it felt for human men, given their obsession with having it.

But sex with Josephine finally made me understand that desire that was more like a need.

It had been overwhelming.

I'd barely come to terms with that idea.

Then she'd flipped over.

And that look.

Fuck, that look.

I'd never lost control over myself during sex. I didn't even think it was a possibility for me to Change from an orgasm. I had been so consumed with the other sensations that I hadn't noticed my tongue, my horns, my fingertips.

Josephine sure had, though.

I'd never had to see that look on someone's face before. Protecting our true identity had been of the utmost importance. Who knew what kind of punishment we would endure should hell—or heaven, for that matter—find out that we'd exposed ourselves to the humans.

I imagined, though, that the look of pure and utter panic, fear, and disgust wouldn't have bothered me as much on anyone else's face.

Then she'd screamed. Actually screamed in horror at seeing me only partially Changed.

I'd told myself it was just the shock of it as I slipped on pants then followed her across the hall. But then I'd found her behind two locked doors.

As if that wasn't bad enough, she'd fucking thrown up.

Thrown up because of my true form.

Thrown up because she'd let me put my evil hands on her.

I didn't recognize the piercing sensation in my chest as I stood there on the other side of that door.

But by the time I'd gotten downstairs, had ripped the drink out of Drex's hand, and thrown it back to feel the burn he'd always been so fond of, bits of fiction and music and poetry came rushing back to my mind. Men and women describing exactly what I'd felt listening to Josephine get sick because she'd slept with me.

"That bad, huh?" Drex asked, smirking at me.

"The fuck are you talking about?" I asked, going back to grab the bottle. I couldn't get drunk. I couldn't even imagine what being drunk felt like to the humans, but the burn was at least distracting to the pain in my chest.

"This place has thick walls," he said, still smirking at me. "And I still heard that headboard slamming against the wall. Color me surprised to find out you're suddenly more of a 'do as I say, not as I do' sort of leader."

"Don't fucking test me right now, Drex," I growled, sucking down some of the alcohol right from the bottle.

"Didn't make her come, huh?" he asked, always the sort to stick a finger in an open wound. "Didn't think I'd heard any screams. Losing your touch, man."

"The fuck did I say?" I roared, grabbing him around the neck, lifting him up out of his seat as the Change came upon me again.

"The fuck is going..." Ly started, he and Seven coming to a stop just inside the library door.

"Ace, man, the fuck?" Seven asked, moving forward, watching me with concerned eyes.

"What'd he do this time?" Ly asked, getting an eye roll from Drex.

"What are you doing?" Lenore's voice joined the others, rushing forward, reaching out for my wrist with her hand, burning me.

She'd gotten a lot better at controlling her powers. So much so that she could call it on demand these days, not just when she was scared or angry.

I might have been immortal, but a third-degree burn still hurt like a mother fucker. It was intense enough for me to drop Drex, to let out a string of curses.

"What is going on?" Lenore demanded, looking around.

"You wanna tell them, or should I?" Drex asked, not intimidated.

After hundreds of years of disagreements with each other, often coming to blows with one another, it took a lot for any of us to get cowed because of a small disagreement.

"Tell us what?" Ly demanded, gaze moving to me.

But I couldn't find the words as I tried to find some self-control, force the Change back.

"He fucked the nurse," Drex supplied.

"And?" Ly asked, confused.

I didn't want to tell them.

But I also had to.

"The nurse knows."

"About what? About us?" Seven asked, tone going grim.

"Well, about me," I supplied, feeling my horns going back in, my tongue coming together.

"Well, shit," Drex said, dropping back down into his seat, eyes far away.

"I'm not sure why that changes anything," Bael said, seeming to come out of nowhere. "The plan was always to kill her. She won't have any contact with the outside world while she heals Red. What's the problem?"

The problem was, the idea of her looking at me like that again. Day in and day out until Red was better. The problem was now that I'd gotten a taste of her, I wanted more, but she got sick at the idea of my hands touching her.

"The problem is, she's locked herself in Red's bathroom, and shows no signs of coming back out," I supplied, trying to keep my tone even. Shit was bad enough, I didn't need them knowing my real reason for being so off.

"She has to eat," Seven reasoned. "She will come out eventually."

"Once she calms down, I will go talk to her," Lenore supplied.

"Yes, because learning that not only do demons exist, but witches do as well, will certainly help the situation," I drawled, getting an eye roll from her.

"I'm the only woman here that can talk to her. It might help. I don't have to say anything about being a witch. Or, you know, part demon myself."

"Do what you got to do," I invited, pushing through the crowd in the doorway, making my way back upstairs, closing myself in my room that still smelled like sex. The sheets were still bunched up where her hands had grabbed them as she came. "Fuck," I hissed, pacing the length of my room, trying to force my thoughts to calm, so I could focus.

I didn't manage that.

And when exhaustion finally called me to bed, I had vivid dreams of her.

She didn't come out the next day.

She didn't, it seemed, even check on Red.

And she certainly hadn't touched the food Lenore and Minos had brought up to her twice that day.

Daemon had even run to the store to pick up various

items he'd heard Josephine mention while she'd cooked herself food.

Even with her favorites there for her, she refused to eat.

She'd rather starve than take anything from us.

That realization made another of those stabbing sensations pierce my chest.

"Just break the fucking door down," Drex suggested, shrugging. "She's only good to us for taking care of Red. She's not doing that. So force her out. Fuck what she thinks about it."

"I'm not so sure she's not checking on Red," Lenore said, drawing my attention. "Red was on the opposite side this morning as she was last night. I mean, I haven't been paying that close of attention, but Red doesn't seem to be writhing around anymore. I don't see how she would have gotten onto her other side unless someone else rolled her there."

"So then, there's no problem," Drex concluded.

"Except humans die if they don't eat," Minos reminded him.

"She will eat eventually," Drex said, shrugging. "She might be stubborn, but humans have a strong survival instinct. I mean, they cannibalize each other when they need to," he added, shrugging. "Besides, if she doesn't make it, we can just get another one. We weren't planning on keeping her on forever."

A low, growling sound moved through my chest, loud enough for Minos and Ly to look at me curiously, but, luckily, no one else noticed.

"And if that is all settled, I am heading out," Drex announced. "Want me to take the little shit with me to keep him out of everyone's hair? If I hear him complain about not getting any pussy while we are on lockdown one more time, I am going to punch a hole through the core of the Earth to send him back to hell myself."

"Did I hear someone call my name? Daemon asked, appearing out of nowhere, clearly shamelessly eavesdropping.

"Yeah, take him. But watch him," I demanded, giving Drex a hard look. I didn't need to say it. After all these years, he knew what I was trying to get across.

We don't need issues with any more supernaturals.

"Oh, he doesn't need to watch me, boss man. I'll keep myself occupied and out of trouble under some pretty lady's skirt," Daemon said, giving me a smirk before making his way out of the front door. Drex followed behind, letting out a sigh.

"So what about Red?" Aram asked, moving into Drex's old seat.

"What about Red?" I asked him.

"Why isn't she healing? Who would have done this to her? And why?"

"Fuck if I know," I admitted, hating the words even as they came out, but there was no way around them anymore. I'd consulted all my books. I couldn't find a single reason a demon would be suffering this long. Or would lose their minds at all. "You got any insight?" I asked, looking at Bael since he'd been in hell most recently.

"You know how it is down there. Different crews. We don't usually attack each other, but shit happens."

"She had no crew," Aram told him. "We're her crew."

That was both true... and not.

We were her crew on Earth after we'd all somehow gotten ourselves sucked up here and stuck. Before then, none of us had really known one another.

"We're her crew now. We weren't always her crew," I reminded them. "She was under Marceaus," I clarified, looking back at Bael.

"Marceaus?" Bael asked, brows drawing together.

"Yes. Why? What aren't you saying?" I demanded.

"Marceaus is a legend."

"Why does that sound past tense?" Seven asked.

"Because no one has seen Marceaus in a generation," Bael said. "Lucifer himself has been pissed since he had disappeared. Marceaus was one of his favorites. One of the most ruthless bastards anyone had ever met."

My gaze slid to Ly, seeing reflected what I already had swirling through my mind.

"Marceaus has to be here," Aram said.

"Yeah, that's what everyone is thinking now," Ly agreed. Then, he looked at me. "How much older is Marceaus than you?"

"A lot," I confirmed.

"Could he know something?" Aram asked.

"We'd have to find him and ask," Seven concluded. "What do you think?" he asked, looking at me.

"I think it's a big fucking world," I told him. "I think that if he came up here a generation ago, he could have acclimated just about anywhere."

"We could put some feelers out," Aram said, hopeful, not anywhere near ready to give up on healing his friend.

"Yeah," I agreed, if for no other reason, than to get some of them out of the way. "You, Seven, and Bael should head out after you've packed and put a plan together."

"You want *us* to put the plan together?" Seven clarified, looking confused. And why shouldn't he? I'd never let them lead up missions without any direction before.

"Yeah. Stay out of trouble with the law. Stay away from any unfriendly supernaturals. And keep in touch."

The men shared a look. Aram was anxious. Seven was determined to prove he could handle it. And Bael, well, Bael was his usual closed-down mask.

"Do you really think he would give a shit about Red after all this time?" Ly asked, getting an elbow from Lenore who may have loved him as he was, but never stopped trying to remind him to be a little kinder.

"I don't know. She talked about him all the time like they had a close mentor/mentee relationship." That she clearly wanted to mean more. "Women of our kind aren't common, so he would have taken extra time with her. Hopefully, it was enough that he would at least offer some insights if he has any."

"We should have told them to pick up Daemon on their way," Ly suggested.

"He's a liability on the road without the rest of us around to rein him in," I said, shrugging. "If he ends up liking the club, we can sic him on Drex most nights."

"I thought you weren't a fan of the club," Ly said, brow raising.

"I'm not. But we have bigger problems right now."

"Problems like the nurse?" he pressed.

"Yes, her starving to death would be inconvenient at best."

"Yeah, that must be the problem," Ly agreed, shaking his head, grabbing Lenore, and making their way out of the room.

"What?" I asked as Minos gave me a long, hard look.

"I... you know what? Nothing," he said, shrugging, and going off to his room to blast his sad music, like usual.

Another day went by that Josephine didn't eat.

But on the third night, I snuck into Red's room, hiding in the dark of her closet, waiting to see if what Lenore said was true, that she found a couple minutes a night to come in and care for her patient still.

I'd just about given up.

It was that moment just before dawn when the sky was still dark, but you could hear some birds already waking up for their morning.

It was probably the one part of the day when none of us were awake, too late for the others, and a little bit too early for me.

That was when the door lock disengaged, then the door cracked open.

Her head appeared, looking around first, then rushing out, giving the food on the plate outside the bathroom door one mournful look before she got to Red, feeling for a temperature, checking the wounds, forcing her medicine down her throat, and then rolling her onto her other side.

With that, she made her way back to the bathroom, pausing, then dropping down beside the plate, grabbing handfuls of cold food, finally proving Drex right. She didn't have the willpower to starve to death.

"If you weren't so stubborn, you could have eaten it when it was warm," I said, getting a shocked gasp out of her as she tried to get up, get back into her tiled sanctuary.

But I was faster, stepping into the doorway just as she got inside, grabbing the door, preventing her from closing it.

"You should let me explain," I suggested, trying to keep my tone even.

"I don't need an explanation," she said, taking steps backward, wanting as much distance from me as possible. "You're evil."

"Yes," I agreed, nodding.

"You have no soul."

"That goes hand-in-hand with the evil part, so yes."

"You're not even going to try to deny it?"

"What use is there for that? You've seen it with your own eyes. You're not stupid."

"I slept with a, with a, *demon*," she said, spitting the word like a curse.

"Yes, you did. I don't see how that changes anything, though."

"You're not human," she snapped.

"That's both true and untrue," I said. "I have human flesh. My body functions like any normal man's does."

"You have horns."

"Occasionally. Usually when I'm angry," I clarified. "And, apparently, when I have sex with you."

"Just me?" she asked. "No, don't answer that. It doesn't matter. It is never going to happen again."

"Yes, just you. I've been around for a long time, Josephine. I've known a lot of women. That has never happened before."

"What does that mean?"

"Honestly, I don't know."

"Did you... did you do something to me?"

"Something like what?" I asked, brows furrowing.

"Like impregnate me like a *Devil's Due* situation?" she asked, looking ashen at the very idea.

"You mean did I put a demon baby inside you? No, Josephine. I wore a fucking condom, remember?"

"Well, I don't know how that works," she said, waving toward my crotch.

"It works similarly to the typical man you're used to. Except I can only impregnate when I intend to. And I didn't," I added when she didn't look convinced. "I know your movies and film make it seem like all we do is come here and knock up unsuspecting women, but that's not how it works."

"How does it work then? Why don't you do that?"

"Because there's no reason to. We don't have typical family structures. There's no real drive to carry on our lineage unless we Claim a human woman. And that rarely happens." Except, not as rarely as it used to, it seemed.

"I don't understand."

"Claiming is, in a way, involuntary. Something in us reacts to a certain woman and Claims her. Lycus and Lenore have that. It means he is attached to her for eternity. He would do anything to protect her, to keep her happy. Even if Lenore had rejected him, the Claiming would be a part of him."

"It sounds like love," she said, shaking her head at me.

"Love is a choice," I countered.

"No, it's not."

"Sure it is. That's how you can fall into and out of it. You choose that. There is none of that with Claiming. We can't fall out of it. It is a forever part of us."

To that, her gaze fell, inspecting the tiles on the floor for a moment before looking back up. "It doesn't matter. That all doesn't matter."

"What does then?"

"You're a demon!" she shrieked before shrinking back like she thought I might charge at her.

"Yes, I am. It doesn't change anything."

"It changes everything!"

"How so? I've been this way since we met. The only difference now is that you know. Nothing has changed."

"What do you want from me?"

"The same thing I've wanted from the beginning. For you to help Red."

"Red is one too, isn't she?" she asked, the dread in her voice letting me know that she hadn't considered that before.

"Yes. We all are. Well, Lenore only partly."

"Partly? How can you be partly demonic?"

"Look, it's a lot," I told her. "If you want the information, I will give it to you. I will answer your questions," I offered, knowing the outcome would be the same regardless, even if an increasingly disproportionate part of me hated the idea of that being her fate. "But you have to come out of this fucking bathroom. You have to eat. There's no reason for you to be miserable."

"I slept with a demon, so, yeah, there is," she mumbled under her breath.

"Hey," I called, moving forward, snagging her chin, forcing it up. "Enough, okay? E-fucking-nough of that. You fucked *me*. It doesn't matter what I am."

"Does it... hurt your feelings?" she asked, brows scrunching. "That I feel this way?"

"We don't have feelings. Not the way you do."

"It seems like you're upset."

Even as she was saying it, I could see what she was saying. It was in the tension in my jaw, in the churning sensation in my stomach.

I was upset.

Offended.

Hurt.

Or some combination of the three.

It was hard to tell after so long without having to deal with most pesky human emotions, save for maybe the ones that came more naturally to my kind— frustration and anger.

But there they were, unmistakable, undeniable.

"If I am, that is something new for me too," I admitted to her, feeling oddly laid bare. This was what vulnerability felt like. I'd never truly wrapped my head around the concept before. "Come on," I said, dropping her chin, taking a few steps back. "Come out of here. Go back to normal. I'll leave you alone if you want. Or, if you would rather, I can educate you. But come out. Sleep on the couch instead of the floor—"

"Bathtub," she corrected, waving, making me turn and find a collection of towels and washcloths piled in the small space.

"That's even worse," I told her, shaking my head. "Sleep on the couch. Eat your food. Think about what you want. Then let me know, okay?" I asked, making my way out of the bathroom, giving her space.

She gave me a tight nod.

"Okay."

"Okay," I agreed. "I'll get Minos to make you something fresh," I said, waving at the food.

"Alright. Thanks," she added, not taking any steps further.

Until I was out of the bedroom, in the hall.

I had a feeling I knew what she was going to want.

Me as far away from her as possible.

It shouldn't have mattered.

But, I found as I sat up all night going over it, it mattered.

It mattered more than anything I could remember anything mattering.

Chapter Thirteen

Jo

It felt like a lifetime ago that I was worried about my new co-workers, about cutting my hair, about maybe getting a new pet.

I had been so much more naive then.

I felt so much older now.

Now that I knew how the world really worked, that demons walked among us, that they didn't look like twisted creatures out of nightmares or horror movies.

Oh, no.

They looked like very attractive human beings.

I'd noticed some things in the couple of days after I emerged from the bathroom to try to find some semblance of normal again. Like the fact that Minos and Ly and Daemon all had the same flecks of red in their eyes that Ace did, just in different patterns. They were all warm. You could feel it from several inches away.

And there was a chilliness to the way they engaged with me that must have been because of their soullessness.

I guess I had been able to overlook all these things because I had nothing to compare them to.

Now, though, it was all glaringly obvious.

I kept finding myself looking for other things about them that was different from me, from us, from the human race.

Since they weren't freaking *human*.

Unfortunately, they all seemed to be under strict instructions not to come too close to me, to linger long. They came in, brought me food, removed old dishes, helped me with Red, and—in the case of Daemon— came in to clean.

"Do you enjoy cleaning?" I found myself asking on the fourth day after I was out of the bathroom, watching Daemon scrub the sink wearing a pair of ridiculous pink cleaning gloves. I knew they came in yellow and even blue, but he was always wearing pink for some reason.

"I can't say that I do, pretty lady," he said, giving me his signature playboy smile.

"Then why are you the one always doing it?"

"I think that answer is two-fold. On one side, I think they all believe I am the least threatening of our kind to come in here for any length of time. On the other, they like making me do all the chores around here."

"You're all evil," I said, shrugging.

"True," he agreed. "But before you knew that, did you hate us all?"

"You kidnapped me."

"You talked to me like a friend in the kitchen while you cooked. Even though we'd kidnapped you."

"Clearly, I have not been thinking straight," I said, tone clipped, a large part of me determined to despise them all, even if they weren't currently giving me a reason to.

"Do you want to try it again?" he asked. "An experiment of sorts?" he added.

"What do you mean?"

"I mean, now you know what we are. Let's go down to the kitchen. You can make yourself something to eat. I will talk to you like I did last time. And then you can decide if you despise me for no good reason—aside from the kidnapping thing which was a factor even then—or maybe see if you're being judgmental over something we can't control."

"You might not be able to control being demons, but you can control walking around Earth, pretending to be men."

"We actually don't. We're stuck here," Daemon told me, pulling off the pink gloves, slipping them into the cleaning bucket under the sink cabinet. "We have been for a while. Well, Red and the others much longer than Bael and me. We didn't choose to be here—though now that I am here, I would pick it over and over—and we can't just go back. We have to be here. So we make the best of it that we can. Including flirting with pretty women," he said, giving me a boyish smile.

"Why can't you go back?"

"Because we weren't supposed to be here in the first place. Something to do with the balance of power. I don't really know. Ace is the expert. Come on, ask me questions while you cook. You're looking skinny," he said, grimacing.

I should have stayed put.

I knew it was what was going to allow me to stay objective, to stay angry.

But I'd been in the room left alone with my own thoughts, going half-crazy, for days.

So I accepted.

And I found the pantry and fridge much fuller than the last time. I actually got to make myself boxed macaroni and cheese, eating the entire thing by myself while Daemon prattled on and on about his adventures since coming to "the human plane" a little over a year and a half before.

"Hey, Daemon?" I asked as he immediately started washing my dishes for me.

"Yeah, pretty lady?"

"Can you bring me to Ace?" I asked, then rushed to clarify. "He said that if I wanted to know more about, well, you know... all of you, that I could come to him, and he would tell me."

"I can do that," he agreed. "Here, you will probably need some coffee," he said, pouring two cups. "It's going to be a lot," he clarified.

With that, he led me through to the front of the house, passing the second mug he'd been carrying that I'd thought was his into my free hand. "And this is where we part," he said, giving me an encouraging smile. "Go get your education on," he added, giving me a little nudge before going back toward the kitchen, leaving me with nothing else to do but move into the library.

That was where I found Ace, sitting in on the tufted leather couch, wearing his usual grandpa sweater, holding a book open in his lap.

Seeming to sense my presence, his gaze lifted slowly, pinning me with his intense gaze.

It sounded completely irrational even in my own head, but I could have sworn he looked pleased. And relieved.

"I, ah, I asked Daemon to bring me here," I explained, shuffling my feet. "He made some good points that made me think."

"Daemon did?" he asked, brow raising.

"I was as shocked as you," I admitted, getting a lip twitch from Ace. "Is that for me?" he asked, nodding toward the extra mug in my hand.

"Oh, ah, yeah. Daemon made it," I explained, not wanting him to think I was thinking about him. Even though I absolutely had been, whether I wanted to or not. And when I tried to suppress the thoughts, they just came back with a vengeance when I fell asleep.

Moving forward, I held out the mug. When Ace reached for it, his big hand slid over mine. And I hate to admit it, but there was no denying the electric shock I felt through my system at his touch.

If I wasn't completely mistaken, Ace seemed to feel it too, his body stiffening, his jaw going tight. "So," he said, pulling the mug from my hand. "You want to learn."

"Yes," I admitted.

"Okay," he said, waving toward the other side of the couch. "Have a seat."

So I did.

And he launched into it.

Daemon had been right. There was a lot to it. So much so that we'd barely scratched the surface by the end of that first day.

By the second, I was actively asking questions.

By the third, the concept stopped feeling so scary because they were no longer so foreign.

And, really, it all threw a lot of what I thought I knew about the nature of good and evil on its head. Because, yes, there was hell and there were demons. But the purpose of that place and those demons was to make people pay in the afterlife for things they often got away with on Earth. A cosmic justice system, if you will. Demons didn't come to Earth to rape and impregnate us. Even though Ace and his club all did do evil work while they were here, all they did was bring the evil to the surface.

"No," he told me, shaking his head. "It doesn't work if they are mostly good. Everyone has a little bit of wickedness in them. But we don't deal in slashing your cheating husband's tires type of shit. The worst thing you have ever done is the nicest thing others have done. Look at it that way, and it isn't so scary. Everyone gets their comeuppance for being complete and utter dicks while they are here. And the punishment fits, too."

He'd touched on all of that as well. The circles of hell, the levels of torment.

"Where did you fall?" I asked, catching him off-guard.

"Hm?"

"When you worked down there, where did you work? Which level of evil did you punish?"

"Me and Ly and Bael, we all worked pretty high up. Serial killers and rapists were our forte."

"What is worse than that?"

"Pedophiles. Mass murderers. People who steal the parking space you were clearly turning into..."

A surprised laugh bubbled up and burst out, surprising us both. "Oh, my God. Was that a joke?" I asked, smiling.

"Things had taken a serious turn there. Figured I'd lighten it up a bit."

"Well, color me impressed. I wasn't sure you had a discernible sense of humor," I teased. "But I guess that makes sense. With you and Ly and Bael."

"How so?"

"Because you're all...colder," I decided. It was the kindest word I could come up with. "Whereas Aram and Seven and Daemon are almost more, I don't know, human. Where did Drex and Minos fit in?"

"Just below us. Wife-beaters, gang shit."

"But then what did Aram and Seven and Daemon deal with?"

"Oh, the other kinds of assholes most people deal with on a daily basis. Asshole bosses who cop a feel, those who abuse their power, people who could have helped others and chose not to. Lower level stuff."

"So, what about those who sleep around a lot or covet their neighbors' nice new car?" I asked, remembering certain rules very clearly.

"If you do it and you are repentant for it, you don't need to worry about us sticking hot pokers in your eye-sockets, Josephine. We handle the people who did what they did and don't give a fuck about who they hurt doing it."

And that was fair, wasn't it?

People who hurt others should have to pay for it.

For that to happen, those like Ace had to exist to exact that punishment.

No, he wasn't human.

No, he didn't have the same feelings as we did.

But that didn't mean he was someone I needed to fear.

You know, anymore than I had to with the whole kidnapping and held captive thing.

Though, let's face it, I wasn't being treated like crap—tossed in a basement somewhere and made to starve and freeze. Most of the bad things that had happened to me since "meeting" them were things I'd done to myself.

I had gone out into the cold and nearly died.

I had chosen not to eat and to sleep in the cold, hard bathroom.

I'd, technically, even been the one to hit my own head.

I wasn't trying to victim-blame myself, but all things said and done, they hadn't treated me badly. Honestly, I think I would have been much more abused at the hands of your average, everyday human kidnappers than I had been by the actual demonic ones I was stuck with.

"What are you thinking about?" Ace asked, snapping me out of my swirling thoughts.

"That for someone evil, you haven't done evil things to me," I admitted, shrugging.

To that, he leaned forward, putting his book on the coffee table, and I could have sworn he mumbled under his breath something that sounded a heck of a lot like *I'm not sure I could even if I wanted to*.

But he immediately spoke again before I could ask. "Is there anything else you want to know?"

"Are you going to kill me?" I asked.

There.

Point-blank.

It was the one question I'd had swirling through my head for days, weeks at this point, I think. It was getting harder to keep track of time.

I saw the answer to that in his jaw before he could even say it, making my stomach twist, my heart speed up.

"Don't," he demanded, reaching out to grab my wrist just as the thought formed to bolt, to run, to get the hell away from them. Even if it meant dying by the elements. Better at my own hands than theirs, I felt. "You didn't let me answer."

"I can see the answer," I snapped, trying to pull my arm away, only managing to yank him forward, closer to me, towering over me as I leaned back against the arm of the couch.

"You can see part of the answer," he corrected.

"There is no part to this. Either you kill me or you don't, there's no in-between with life."

"The plan was to kill you," he admitted, making my heart squeeze in my chest, a tightness to close around my neck, cutting off my air. "But that isn't the... I can't do that anymore," he told me, shaking his head.

In that moment, I wanted to loathe him, this man who so casually considered taking my life.

But when I looked at his face, all I could see there was confusion and vulnerability, and maybe even something else. Something I didn't want to name because a part of me wasn't ready to accept it yet.

I swallowed past the lump in my throat, wetting my lips. "What changed?"

"You know what changed," he shot back, the grip on my wrist loosening a bit, his thumb stroking across the underside gently.

I knew it wasn't supposed to. I knew he was evil. I knew he should have repulsed me. But there was no denying that the soft touch sent tingles up my arm, then across my chest.

"There's... there's nothing," I tried to claim, but couldn't force my lips to spill the rest of the lie.

"Yes, there is," he countered. "There's something here."

"There can't be," I insisted, feeling his hand slip, fingers sliding between mine, lifting my arm above my head as his body shifted, his knee pressing between my thighs, forcing me to turn until I was lying on the couch, his body hovering above mine. Not touching, but so close. Dangerously close.

My damn traitorous heart fluttered in my chest at the intensity I saw in his eyes.

"There can be," he countered, leaning down, pressing his lips into the side of my neck. The shiver that coursed through me told me that while my mind was conflicted, my body most certainly wasn't. "If you want there to be," he added, teeth gently nipping my earlobe.

"It's not that simple," I insisted, feeling my brain already getting slow and foggy with desire as his tongue traced up my ear.

"What's complicated?" he asked.

"You're my captor," I reminded him, taking a measured breath, but feeling it shake in my chest.

To that, he pressed back enough to look down at me, his eyes glowing red with his desire. "If you want to leave, leave," he offered.

"You're not going to let me leave."

"You want to leave, go," he said, shrugging as he sat back on his heels. I felt the loss of his hand in mine more than I should have, enough to almost make me reach for his again.

"And, what, you'll chase me down?" I asked.

"No."

"You can't let me go. I know about you. I can tell people."

"You won't," he said, shaking his head.

"Why not?"

"Because you're not stupid," he said, giving me a humorless laugh. "These days, when people start talking about fucking a demon, they get sent to a psych ward."

He wasn't exactly wrong about that, was he? I'd certainly come across several delusional individuals in my time in emergency rooms. And when they muttered about things that didn't exist—or things I thought didn't exist—someone always called for a psychological evaluation, usually ending with a hold and, eventually, medication.

I couldn't help but wonder if I'd ever disbelieved someone when they'd told me their story, when it actually turned out to be true.

"I could go to people who would believe me."

"Good luck finding any these days," he said. "I've had actual conversations with holy people in my time. They never suspected a thing. And a lot of them these days don't take things quite as literally as they were once written."

"You'd really let me go?" I asked, searching his face for any small tell.

"I would really let you go. If you wanted to go."

Of course I wanted to go.

Right?

"At any time?" I asked, somehow knowing that right now was not it.

"At any time," he agreed. "I would even drive you to the airport."

"The airport?" I asked. "How far did you take me?"

"Across the country," he told me, tone unapologetic.

"I, ah, I wouldn't be, like, you know, be making a deal with the devil, right?" I clarified, deciding in a situation such as this, the fine print was very, very important.

To that, I got a smile.

An actual, genuine smile.

Not a smirk, or a sneer.

A freaking *smile* from this grumpy man.

"No, Josephine, your soul is yours to keep," he said, tone lighter than I had ever heard it, playful, teasing. And, damn, it was a beautiful thing from such a serious man.

"You promise?"

"Yes, I promise," he said, eyes going just the slightest bit soft. "So, we're agreed? You are free to leave at any time. But you're also free to stay as long as you want?"

The issue was probably important enough to require actual thought. But did I do that? No, no I did not.

"We're agreed," I said, giving him what felt like a wobbly smile.

But it didn't last long.

"Thank fuck," he hissed, coming down on me, lips sealing to mine. Hard. Hungry.

And with that, any thoughts about him being anything other than a man I desired slipped away.

There was no hesitation as my legs wrapped around his hips, pulling him more firmly against me, feeling his hardness press into me. I greedily writhed against him, needing the friction, as Ace's hand slipped under my shirt, cupping my breast as that growling noise I liked too much moved through him.

His forefinger and thumb closed around my nipple, twisting, squeezing, then rolling, making my hips buck up against him as the need for release grew.

"Ace," I whimpered, fingers dragging his shirt up his back, awkwardly yanking it up over his head, getting a little chuckle out of him as he pressed back again, looking down at me as he got rid of the shirt.

I might have been impatient for release, but I took my sweet time looking over his chest, his stomach, those muscles of his Adonis belt that disappeared into his pants.

I folded up toward him, my hands going to his pants, working them free, reaching inside, and pulling out his cock, slipping him inside my mouth before Ace could even guess my intentions, getting a surprised hiss out of him as I worked down his hard length.

His hand went to the back of my neck, keeping me deep, then thrusting into my mouth.

I'd always liked having control during oral.

But letting Ace have it? It was something forbidden and sexy.

My head tipped back slightly, my eyes opening, finding him watching me intensely as he fucked my mouth.

"Fuck," he hissed, taking a shaky breath. "No," he said when he tried to pull away and my hands sank into his ass to try to hold on. "It's my turn," he clarified, yanking back, grabbing the backs of my knees, and flipping me onto my back on the couch.

My pants and panties were off before I could even suck in a proper breath. Then his hands were spreading my thighs, and he was between them, devouring me with the same sort of enthusiasm as I'd felt for him.

He drove me right up and through my orgasm. Which, admittedly, didn't take very long at all thanks to the sleepless nights that I'd spent writhing around on my little couch having vivid memories of his hands on me, him inside me, leaving me feeling constantly turned-on and anxious for release.

Before the waves could even fully finish crashing, he was off of me, grabbing a condom, and slipping it on. Returning to me, his hands sank into my sides, lifting, and flipping me until I was on my knees, my hands braced on the armrest of the couch.

Ace's knee pressed mine apart, and then he was slamming inside me.

Hard.

Deep.

A surprised moan escaped me as his hand grabbed my hip, using it to slam me back into him as he began to thrust.

There was nothing slow or explorative about this.

This was pure, primal hunger.

And I was right there with him, my walls closing tight around his cock as he drove me quickly up to another crest.

His other hand shot out, closing around the front of my throat, using it to draw me backward against his chest, but his fingers stayed there, cutting off a small amount of air, just until my face felt warm, my lips a little tingly.

"Come," he demanded, voice as rough as my nerve endings felt, poised there at that precipice for an agonizing moment before shoving me off of it, leaving me free falling into my orgasm, crying out his name as I came, feeling Ace's body jolt as he came with me, the tips of his talons digging into my throat.

I thought it would sicken me to feel that Change again, bringing back the horror and confusion of the last time.

But instead, I felt another small surge of waves move through me, leaving me gasping for air as Ace's arms went around me, holding me to him, or I was sure I would have face-planted forward.

My breathing was ragged as I leaned my head back against Ace's shoulder. A smile tugged at my lips as Ace leaned down and pressed a sweet kiss to the side of my head.

Ace.

Sweet.

They were two words that shouldn't have gone together, yet there was no denying that they did. Just this once, at least.

"We have to move," I said a moment later, feeling some semblance of order returning to my body.

"No, we don't."

"Someone could walk by at any moment," I reminded him.

"So?" he asked. "Hate to break it to you, Josephine, but anyone in the house just heard you cry my name when you came, so everyone already knows."

I felt the warmth flood my cheeks at the idea of them hearing me, knowing what we were doing. Even if I'd heard several of the others going at it with women in my short stay at their house.

"Yes, but knowing and *seeing* are two completely different things," I insisted, feeling very exposed from the waist down.

"Alright," Ace said, grudgingly sliding out of me, retrieving his pants, then tossing mine at me. "I'll be right back," he added, walking out of the library and down the hall.

And it was right that moment that I knew for sure there had been no ploy to get me to sleep with him again, to trust him.

Because he'd left me alone.

None of the others seemed to be hanging around.

He was in the bathroom.

I could get right up and walk out the front door.

Maybe I should have done exactly that.

But, instead, I got into my pants, and I walked back toward the kitchen, making us each a cup of coffee.

I heard the bathroom door open, footsteps going toward the library.

And then, a slamming sound followed by the ear-splitting roar of, "Fuck!"

Panic left me frozen there for a moment as I heard the others come running, demanding to know what was going on.

"She's fucking gone," he snapped at them, voice more demonic than human.

It should not have been sexy.

And yet.

Grabbing the cups, I rushed back down the hall, moving into the doorway to find the others assembled, watching Ace as he seemed to almost flicker in and out of the Change.

"I, ah, yeah," I agreed, seeing all their heads turn in my direction. "To get coffee," I added, holding the mugs up.

I would never forget the look I saw cross Ace's face right then. It was the look I'd seen on faces of family members who came rushing in after hearing their loved ones were in some sort of serious accident, when they'd learned it was all going to be okay.

It was raw, undiluted relief.

Because I hadn't left.

Ace's eyes closed as he took several slow, deep breaths, trying to control the Change.

Feeling oddly like that was a private struggle, my gaze slid instead to Minos, whose gaze felt like it was melting through my skin, it was so intense.

I didn't understand the look in his eyes. I wasn't sure I wanted to. But whatever had caused it to be there made him sigh, shake his head, and walk back out of the room.

"So, we are letting the puppy off her leash?" Daemon asked, shooting me a boyish smile.

"We had a talk," Ace said, looking at him. "She is free to move around as she pleases."

"Are you fucking kidding me?" Drex snapped, making Ace's brow rise.

Granted, I hadn't known the man long, but I knew him well enough to know that look on his face was not one you wanted shot in your general direction. Drex appeared un-cowed, though.

"Jo," Lenore said, using the name I'd told her to call me by since literally everyone in my life always had. Except for Ace. And even when I was trying to deny my irrational connection to him, a stubborn little part of me only wanted him to use my full name like that. "Why don't we go check on Red?" she suggested, turning to me, giving me wide eyes, a universal 'the guys are being ridiculous' look.

"Yeah," I agreed, almost feeling a little sorry for Drex, but only a little. Since he wanted to keep me caged like an animal.

"So, you and Ace," she said, eyes bright. "Sorry, I know. That's private. I just... I've never gotten to talk to a woman about her relationship."

"Ever?" I asked, turning to face her as we moved into Red's room.

"I, ah, didn't Ace tell you about me?"

"Not really, no."

"I come from an all-female coven," she explained.

"You're a *witch*?" I asked, almost feeling a little star-struck. I'd been obsessed with witch TV shows and movies as a teenager. A small part of me always wished they were real, and that I would someday learn I was one myself.

"Partly, yeah. I'm a little bit demon now too," she told me. "Since Ly. So I can live on with him," she explained. "Witches are like humans. Mortal. Longer-lived, but mortal. But anyway, if the women wanted children, they went out into the world and got pregnant, but none of us had relationships."

"So you haven't had anyone to talk to about you and Ly?" I asked, feeling sad for her. I had fond memories of all-night talking sessions with friends and even my mother about boys and men I had been dating, or had even gotten serious with. It was an important part of me learning what I did and didn't want, what was and wasn't behavior I wanted in my life. I couldn't imagine never having had that.

"No. Red... Red left before she and I could really connect. It's been just me and the men since," she said, giving me a look that was both warm and frustrated at the same time. And given what I knew about these men, I could totally understand that.

"Okay," I said, moving to the couch, patting the space next to me. "Tell me about you and Ly," I offered.

She launched into it.

And then asked me about what was going on with Ace.

Before we knew it, it was late, and the yelling down below had stopped.

"That would be Drex heading off to his kinky club," Lenore explained when the front door slammed so hard it sounded like it might have cracked. His bike roared to life a moment later. "I should go check with Ly. Make sure no one is bleeding."

"They actually physically fight?"

"Men," she said, rolling her eyes at me.

"That's fair enough," I agreed, smiling as she made her way to the door.

"This was nice," she declared.

"It was," I agreed, getting up and making my way over to Red, going through the motions of checking her over.

"I can't figure out why she hasn't healed," Ace said, making me jump, turning to find him leaning in the doorway.

"She was horribly abused," I reminded him.

"Yes, but we heal quickly. She should have healed days ago."

"Well, she is healing. That's what is important, right? I think I can take some of these stitches out tomorrow. Some of the bigger wounds could probably use another day or two. But she's getting better. Lenore said you were sending for Mar-Mark..." I could see his name in my head—Marceaus—but couldn't get it right.

"Mar-kay-us," he sounded out for me again. "Yeah. He's older than the rest of us. He might know why she isn't healing. And what is going on with her..." he trailed off, waving at his head.

"Do you think they will find him?"

"I don't think so," he admitted, sounding defeated. "At least not anytime soon. And by the time they do, who knows what will be left?" he said, giving Red a sad look.

"You never know when people will just... snap out of it. It happens all the time. Even sometimes people who the doctors say will never wake up. And, I mean, she isn't even in a coma or anything. Don't get discouraged."

"We're not people, Josephine," he reminded me.

"All the more reason to expect she will pull through. You're not as weak as us puny mortals," I told him, giving him a playful smile, trying to lighten the mood.

"She all set?"

"Until tomorrow morning, yeah," I said. I was going to see if Lenore and I could manage some sort of sponge bath now that she was, by and large, healed.

"Good. Come on," he said, holding an arm out.

"Come where?" I asked, feeling the tiredness hanging around me. I didn't want to learn anything else that night. I just wanted to sleep.

"To bed," he clarified.

"I sleep there," I reminded him, waving toward my couch. I'd long since gotten over neatly folding my blanket on top of my pillow. It still looked the same as it had when I'd crawled out of it earlier.

"Not anymore," he told me, moving further into the hall as I approached.

"Is this so you can keep an eye on me, but give me the illusion of freedom?" I asked, suspicious by nature, and still not entirely sure how much I could trust a creature from hell.

"Josephine, you're going to need to learn to trust me," he told me, sighing a bit, forcing some of the tension out of his jaw. "But I don't want you in my bed because I want to keep an eye on you. I want you in my bed so you're comfortable. And so I can wake you up and fuck you first thing in the morning," he told me, his voice a dark promise that made my sex clench hard.

"Well," I said, swallowing hard, following him into the hall. "In that case," I told him, smiling as he dropped an arm down over my shoulders, and led me into his room.

He made good on his promises, too.

I slept like a baby nestled up on his chest.

And I woke up to his hands already starting to stoke a little fire in my body.

A girl could get used to it.

And I did. Whether that was smart or not. Whether that meant I genuinely did have some sort of Stockholm Syndrome or something similar. Whether or not it was good for my mortal soul.

I got used to it.

To him.

To the strange and wonderful new dynamic growing between us.

Then, one night just about a week later, everything changed.

Chapter Fourteen

Ace

I woke up every morning in a panic, sure she would be gone.

I didn't know what to think about it.

Judging by the sideways looks Ly and Minos kept sending me, they thought I'd Claimed her. But there hadn't been any signs of that.

So I didn't understand the feelings coursing through me. True to form, I'd spent many hours trying to convince myself that I was only concerned about her leaving because she now possessed all of our secrets. I hadn't left anything out. At times, when I'd clearly been trying to tiptoe around certain topics, Josephine had asked more questions until she got it all out of me.

While I did have concerns about a human with our secrets, I also knew myself well enough at this point to know it wasn't just that. It was personal.

I went to sleep with her draped over me like a blanket, lending a warmth I'd been seeking for ages, but never found. The contentedness that flooded my chest as I fell asleep was a high that I looked forward to every day. And the idea of that no longer being a factor in my life—her no longer being a part of my life—left me with a skittering heartbeat and a churning stomach.

I'd grown attached to her.

A goddamn human.

Whose entire lifespan would pass in a blink for me.

I wasn't sure what it was about her, either.

Yes, she was beautiful. Yes, she was intelligent. Yes, I found her curiosity and eagerness to learn sexier than I could have anticipated. Yes, I admired her dedication in caring for Red even when she was no longer being forced to.

So, sure, it must have been all those things mixed together. But there was something else as well, something I couldn't put a finger on, something I didn't have words for. It was something *other* and that otherness was what had me so captivated.

I didn't understand it.

In all my years, I'd never felt anything for the humans aside from a general annoyance at their close-mindedness or a sort of detached interest in their evolution through more technological times.

Sure, I felt attraction toward the women I'd slept with over the years. But it was a fleeting thing. An itch that needed scratching.

Even sex with Josephine felt new and, at times, overwhelming. It was something I found myself craving in inopportune moments. I kept expecting to get my fill, to be over it, but it didn't seem to happen. If anything, I just kept wanting it—wanting her—more.

"Why do you always give me that look?" Josephine asked, coming in the bedroom door, holding two mugs of coffee.

I didn't need to ask her what the look was. I could feel it. It was pure and utter relief. Still, I needed to ask, to know if she was gleaning what I'd been feeling.

"What look?"

"I don't know," she admitted. "Like you're shocked or something like that."

"Must be because the woman who nearly died of exposure trying to get away from me is now bringing me coffee."

"Yes, well, clearly, I need to have an intense psychological evaluation," she said, giving me a soft smile as she handed me the mug, climbing over me to curl up at my side and drink her coffee.

"You're not crazy," I insisted, words urgent. Because I needed that to be true. I needed her warmth toward me to be genuine.

Why?

I had no idea.

But it mattered.

"No," she agreed, resting her head on my chest for a second. "I'm not crazy. This situation is, but I'm not." She paused there, something weighing heavy in the air.

"What is it?" I asked, my arm going around her shoulder, fingers sifting through her hair.

"My old life," she started, trying to think of a way to phrase it.

"Do you want to go back to it?" I asked, wondering if she heard the dread I so clearly recognized in my voice.

"No. Well, sort of, but mostly no. I mean, if I'm not welcome—"

"You're welcome," I cut her off. "For as long as you want to be here," I added.

I knew that one day she would be gone. She'd want things I couldn't give her. Normalcy. Weddings and babies and growing old together.

But I tried not to let myself focus on those thoughts too much.

"Okay," she agreed, letting out a slow breath.

"So what 'sort of' is there then?" I asked.

"I have things," she told me. "Well, I guess, I used to have things. In my apartment. If no one has broken in and taken them. Or my landlord hasn't cleared the place."

"You want your shit."

"Yes," she said, smiling over at me. "I want my shit. Red's clothes are, uhm, cold." Which was a nice way of saying that Red liked to show some skin. "And Lenore's are..." She was struggling to find a nice thing to say about all the floor-length skirts.

"Amish," I supplied.

"Something like that," she agreed. "I like, you know, pants."

"Skirts have easier access," I said, sliding my finger up under the one she'd slipped on to go get us coffee, slipping between her thighs, teasing up her pussy.

"That's true," she agreed, sighing as my finger found her clit. "Still," she tried to insist even as her legs spread wider for me, giving me room to thrust two fingers lazily inside her.

"How about you wear skirts and nothing at all for a little while longer, then we can take the long-ass trip out there to get your shit?" I suggested, my cock already rock-solid as her walls pulled my fingers in tighter.

"Mmm," she said, letting me take her coffee cup away, putting it on the nightstand. "Okay," she agreed, hips rocking rhythmically to my thrusts.

"If you had pants on," I said, grabbing her, yanking her up on my lap where her wet pussy slid over my hard cock, "this wouldn't be as easy," I told her, rocking against her cleft as my free hand went into the nightstand.

"You make a good point," she agreed as I slipped on the condom.

"Always so greedy for my cock," I hissed as her hips lifted, and she slid down on my cock as soon as I was done.

"Mmhm," she agreed, already rocking, already driving herself up.

I couldn't claim to have ever felt the urge to slow down sex before, to make it more than what it was, but as she started to get harder and faster, I grabbed her, rolling her under me, and taking over.

Slow.

Measured.

I'd never bought into that shit about sex being about the journey as much as the destination. Sex was always to come. That was the whole point. But, somehow, as the confusion turned to desire, to an almost raw vulnerability on her face, all that mattered was the moment, our bodies moving together, her legs wrapping around my waist, her soft sighs, her arms encircling my neck, pulling me down to press our lips together.

I didn't give a damn about an orgasm right then.

I just wanted to be close to her, to be inside of her, to be a part of her.

"Ace..." she whimpered, her hips wriggling restlessly.

But in that moment, I was too selfish to speed it up for her, to give her what she needed most.

I'd never been quite so in the moment before, so in-tune with someone. I noticed every hitch to her breath, every flex of her fingers on my shoulders, the way her thigh muscles started to shake, the way her voice went from higher-pitched whimpers to lower, deeper moans.

Her walls tightened hard around me, letting me know she wasn't going to wait any longer.

My lips pulled from hers as my hand reached back to grab hers, pinning it to the mattress above her head, holding as her back arched, as her mouth opened in a silent moan, as her walls started a deep throbbing around me.

She came hard and deep and long, milking my orgasm out of me too, leaving me a boneless mass on top of her for a long moment as I struggled to pull myself back together.

"What's the matter?" she asked as I finally found the strength to push back up, and look down at her.

"Nothing's the matter," I said, brows furrowing.

Her hand rose, fingertip tracing over my temple. "You didn't change at all," she told me, voice concerned. Like she was worried, uncertain. Like she possibly thought it may have been a sign that I was losing interest in her.

She wanted answers, but I didn't have any. I didn't know how to tell her that while the primal side of me might not have responded this once, that it hadn't impacted me any less.

"I don't know," I admitted. "Best guess is the Change is more of a primal response," I told her. "And that wasn't primal. That was something different," I said, rolling to my side, pulling her onto hers.

"Oh," she said, jaw softening, tension leaving her body. "That makes sense."

"I'll be right back," I told her, getting out of bed, making my way to the bathroom.

"Hey, Ace?" she called.

"Yeah?"

"Can we go out today?" she asked.

I tried to pretend the 'we' didn't make this strange sensation tingle through my chest, but there was also no denying it.

"Any place in mind?" I called, hoping my voice came out less impacted than I felt.

"Just out," she said, sounding light, easy. "I've been cooped up forever," she added.

And, to her, it probably had felt like that. To me, it seemed like no time at all.

"We can do that," I agreed, coming back out to find her in my spot, drinking her coffee.

"I can see the sights. Now that I know where I am," she added, rolling her eyes at me. "Oh, can we get *food*?"

"You say that like we haven't been feeding you," I said, climbing over her, taking my coffee when she handed it to me.

"No, it's gotten a lot better," she admitted. "How do I explain this to someone who doesn't really care about food?" she asked, pursing her lips.

It wasn't that we didn't care about food. We all used to. Eating had never been much of a thing where we were from, so when we came to the human plane, like many other things, eating had been something we'd all indulged in heavily. And each fifty years or so, the diet would change enough for us all to go through a phase again, testing out the new things humans had come up with. Food-like products that came in packages, were created in labs, not the actual food that came from the ground.

"Sometimes you just need something fatty and greasy that you didn't make yourself," she declared.

"Like pizza?" I asked.

"Yes!" she said, letting out a moan that was damn near sexual. "Exactly like pizza. Let's get pizza."

"We can do that. Anything else?"

"Can we see the ocean? I've seen the west coast, but not the east."

"It will be cold as fuck, but we can do that too."

"And fries."

"I thought you wanted pizza."

"I want pizza *and* fries. We puny mortals need to eat several times a day," she said, giving me a saucy smile. "Before you guys stole me, I used to have bigger boobs and butt, I swear," she added, tsking her tongue.

"In that case, why don't we do some pasta and ice cream?" I suggested, getting a girlish giggle out of her.

"I like the way you think."

I spent the day on pins and needles—and finally understood on a personal level what the humans meant by that turn of phrase—because a part of me was convinced Josephine was looking for the right moment to flag down a stranger, to tell them she'd been kidnapped, to beg for help, to run away from me and never look back again.

I couldn't shake the feeling, even as she told me about her mom, about the childhood she'd once played down like she hadn't struggled, when they clearly had.

It was there when we got a table at a packed pizza place, and she had eyes only for me. Well, only for me until a pile of grease and cheese and bread was put on a plate in front of us. Then I was pretty sure she preferred the pizza to me. At least until she grumbled that I'd let her eat too much and Red's borrowed skirt was too tight.

So we went ahead and picked up some pants. And my stomach was in knots as she tried on different pairs, modeling a few for me, asking me for input. When she dipped back into the changing room area, I was paranoid she wouldn't come back to me. Even though she did.

It was a present worry even when we went to the ocean, and she'd gasped and grabbed my hand. When she showed me the shells she found, holding one up with the glee of a little kid and declared, "This is a mermaid's toenail!"

By the time we swung by some drive-through to get her a greasy meal out of a bag which she ate while dancing around to some atrocious song on the radio, I started to feel some of the tension leave my shoulders.

Something dangerous uncurled through my system, something I could only name hope.

"That was the most fun I've had in a long time," she declared as we started down the long road to the house, the sun already well set. "And I don't just mean since you kidnapped me," she added, sending me a saucy smile as she licked the ice cream cone she swore she didn't have room for. "What?" she asked when she did another slow, deliberate lick while keeping eye-contact.

"You know what," I told her, voice rough.

"Well," she said, licking the corner of her mouth. "If you want to hold this for me," she said, pushing the cone into my hands as she moved up to her knees on the seat, "maybe I can see for myself what," she finished, leaning over the center console of the SUV, pulling my cock out, and sucking me deep.

It was right then that I finally felt the uncertainty leave my body. Because she'd had more than a dozen chances to get away from me. But she chose to come home with me. She chose to come home with me *then go down on me in the front seat of the car in the driveway.*

She didn't want to go anywhere.

She wanted to be right beside me.

And under me.

And on top of me.

But most of all, she wanted to be *with* me.

That was a high I was still riding as we settled in the library with Ly and Lenore. Drex had taken Daemon with him to the club. Minos was off, well, being Minos—probably sulking and listening to sad shit on repeat.

The girls had put their heads together and decided to put on some show about some brothers who hunted down and killed demons. They claimed to fuck with us, but they were clearly into it as Ly openly scoffed at the plots and I zoned out with a book, happy to have Josephine sitting near me, even if we weren't into doing the same thing at all times. A different kind of intimacy, if you will.

It was a perfectly fucking normal evening.

And, at first, when we heard the bikes, I didn't immediately jump to anything negative, figuring maybe the guys had decided to head back early on their little mission.

It wasn't until they got closer that Ly and I started to share unsure looks with each other.

There were too many bikes.

"Turn the TV off," Ly snapped, getting to his feet.

Lenore jumped, dropping the remote, having to scramble for it to turn the show off as the bikes came up the driveway.

"What's going on?" Josephine asked, following me as I got off the couch, going toward the bookshelf to grab the guns we kept stashed there.

Sure, if Ly and I decided to Change, we could tear humans to shreds with our bare hands. But that was a last resort for obvious reasons.

We'd pissed off plenty of people just by being bikers, by making deals that put other clubs out of business, by being assholes as a whole.

Any one of those clubs could come for retribution. We could easily handle that with some gunfire.

"Stay back," I demanded, pushing Josephine behind my back as Ly moved to do the same, even if Lenore wasn't mortal anymore. She could still get hurt. It still mattered to Ly to protect her.

The engines cut.

Footsteps made their way up the path.

They didn't pause to ring, to knock, just charged in like they owned the joint, like they were welcome.

There were what seemed like ten of them in all, coming to a stop inside the doorway.

There was something primal and *otherworldly* about them immediately, something that made me stiffen, that made Josephine let out a startled gasp.

It was that sound that did it.

It pushed past whatever strange boundary that had been in the way, whatever it was that made me flicker, that made me dance around what I think everyone knew was coming.

It was her fear that brought it out of me.

The Change.

But more instantaneously.

And with dramatics.

Meaning a low, feral growl escaped me even as my wings shot out from my skin.

I hadn't felt or seen my wings in so long I'd forgotten how they'd felt like an extension of myself, like extra arms. And one of those wings had wrapped around a startled Josephine encircling her completely.

To that, the leader of the group of men who weren't quite men lifted a brow slowly. Not shocked and not interested, even. It was at once curious and dismissive.

"You've been here too fucking long," he growled.

Growled because that was how his voice sounded. Like a growl.

I didn't recognize him personally.

But he was as tall as I was, but a mountain of a man. Wide, strong, with arms that were bigger than my thighs, a chest that looked like you could bounce shit off of.

His hair was dark, cut short at the sides and slightly longer on the top, there was a matching beard on his tan face, and something about him spoke of what humans would consider Middle Eastern lineage, though he had no accent at all to speak of it.

His eyes were black.

As was the mood that seemed to hang around him.

Cold, lethal, merciless.

Those were words that came to mind immediately.

"Here?" Ly asked, recovering before I did, making me look to see his wings were out as well, but only curled around Lenore, not wrapping her up completely. Not yet anyway. He'd long-since gotten used to his Claiming of his woman. He could control it better.

"Earth. The human plane. Whatever the fuck you want to call it. Not home."

"Home?" I clarified, drawing his gaze over to me again.

"Are we really playing these fucking games? I got shit to do. I don't have time for it."

"Then why are you here?" I asked, voice getting a little more threatening.

"I hear you've been looking for me."

Ly and I shared a quick glance, both of us realizing it at the same time.

This wasn't some biker we pissed off.

It wasn't some supernatural who didn't like us.

No.

This was fucking Marceaus.

The oldest of us.

The most brutal of us.

Red's mentor.

"You're Marceuas?" I asked, feeling the tension leaving my shoulders, letting my wing relax as well, tucking Josephine close, but not blocking her completely.

"Yeah, and as I said, I don't have the fucking time for this. What do you want?"

"Red."

"Red what?" he asked, brows screeching.

"Not what, who," I corrected. "Red. She worked for you. You trained her."

The realization came over him in a wave, making him lose some of the tension.

"I haven't seen her since she disappeared."

"She didn't disappear. She came up here," I explained. "To the human plane. Got sucked up with the rest of us."

A muscle ticked in his jaw. "That fits," he agreed. "What about her? I haven't seen her if you're looking for her."

"We're not looking for her. She's upstairs," I explained. "She went back down when we found an opening," I told him, not wanting to give away our secrets, let any other demons know they could use the witches if they wanted to. We'd been decent enough to them, but I couldn't guarantee all our kind would.

"And she's back?" he asked, confused.

"Yeah. She came back. Fucking battered. Every inch of her whipped. Toenails pulled out."

"*What*?" he barked, all that tension that had fled coming back with vengeance.

"Yeah. We're as confused as you are. But we were looking for you because that's not it."

"How is it not it?"

"She's healed. Very, very slowly," I told him, seeing the confusion we'd felt at witnessing it. "With human medical assistance," I added. "But something else is wrong with her."

"Show me," he demanded, waving his arm out, making his men fall back several steps. "Relax," he added when my wing tightened around Josephine. "I have no fucking use for your little human," he added. The pure indifference in his voice said he wasn't lying. But I kept her tucked at my side as we led him upstairs, leaving Ly and Lenore and Minos—who'd heard the ruckus and emerged in the shadows to keep an eye on things—to watch over Marceaus's men.

I led him into Red's room, stopping halfway in, waving at the bed. "She's been like this since she came up."

"No," Josephine corrected, making Marceaus look at her fully for the first time. "No," she started again, clearing her throat awkwardly. "At first, she was screaming. Non-stop screaming."

"She's still fucking screaming," Marceaus said, jaw ticking.

"What do you mean she's screaming?" I asked, confused.

He didn't answer, though. Instead, he made his way toward the bed, kneeling on the end, whipping off the blankets, and grabbing Red with rough hands, yanking her around.

"Hey," Josephine snapped, trying to charge forward, getting held in place by my wing.

I admired her desire to take care of her patient, but she was a fool if she thought she could stop this man.

Hell, I would be a fool to think I could.

Besides, I didn't think he was trying to hurt her.

He was checking her out, looking at her wounds, making grumbling noises to himself as he inspected every inch of her feet, her legs, thighs, stomach, chest, arms.

Finally, he flipped her onto her stomach, grabbing her hair as he leaned forward.

"What is he doing?" Josephine demanded.

But I had no answers for her.

All I knew was that Marceaus seemed to know what he was doing, was looking for something.

I knew it the second he found it, too.

Because he snarled.

If I hadn't been watching so closely, I would have missed him reaching into his back pocket. I would have missed the knife in his hand.

As it was, I was too slow to say or do anything before he was leaning over Red's body, slicing into her scalp.

"No!" Josephine shrieked, again trying to surge forward.

But it was over.

It was already over.

He'd carved a piece of skin off of her skull.

Then tossed it onto the bed, turning, and making his way back toward the door with bloodied hands.

"Where the fuck are you going?" I raged at him.

"Got shit to handle," he returned in his growling voice.

Like that, he was gone, and Josephine was pulling against my wing, trying to get to Red.

I let her go.

Because I was going in that direction as well.

But while she jumped on the bed to inspect the wound, my focus wasn't on Red herself, but the part of her that Marceaus had cut off.

And there it was.

What we had all missed all along.

The source of her screaming.

Both audible and silent, it seemed.

"What is it?" Josephine demanded, pressing the bedsheet to Red's bleeding wound.

It likely wouldn't bleed for long, though.

Because Marceaus had found the reason she hadn't healed in the first place.

"It's a cross tattoo," I told her, my mouth barely able to get the words out, my jaw was so tight.

"What?"

"A cross," I told her again. "We're evil," I reminded her.

"Oh! Oh," she said, brows furrowing. "Right. Holy things burn. But then... then how did that happen? How could demons do that to her?"

"They couldn't have," I told her. "Don't fucking ask me how, but humans did this. In hell."

Which meant shit had gotten bad down there.

If humans were able to act up.

If they were able to overpower one of us.

"I don't understand," Josephine said.

"Neither do I," I admitted. "Neither do I. But I do know one thing."

"What's that?"

"Red is going to be up and rearing to go in a couple hours at most."

"No."

"Yes, absolutely."

"That's not possible. She's too far gone."

As it turned out, we were both right.

Red woke up just about two hours after her former mentor and his men cleared out.

She'd looked around at us, confused for a moment. Then she'd taken all the information we'd tossed at her while she lounged in bed, her hand pressing absentmindedly at her tattooed spot, the flesh healed back over.

"Wait. Marcaeaus was here?" she asked. "And he's gone?"

That was when Josephine became right.

She woke up.

Then she got dressed.

And she was far, far gone.

Chasing after a man she clearly had a thing or two to say to.

"Are we going to talk about it?" Josephine asked after all the crazy died down, after the men and I had discussed it, had called the others to explain, to tell them to head home.

"Talk about what?" I asked as we sat on the couch in the living room.

"About this," she said, reaching out to stroke her fingers over my wing. The one that was still wrapped protectively around her. "This means you, ah..."

"Claimed you," I supplied, finding the words a little clumsier on my tongue than I would have expected since I'd had hours to realize the same thing, to come to terms with it.

"Yes, Claimed me," she agreed, shooting an uncertain look my way, then focusing on my wing instead.

"It means what I explained to you. I've chosen you. You will always be all the one for me. I will protect you at all costs for the rest of your life. Whether you choose me back or not," I added, thinking of Minos and his unknown woman. The one who wanted nothing to do with him. The one who turned his once lively self into a miserable sack.

"You're immortal," she said, chewing her lower lip.

"Yes," I agreed.

"I'm mortal," she finished.

"Yes, you are."

"So, what, you would choose me and care about me and protect me even when I am white-haired and hunched over and smelling of arthritis cream?"

"Yes, Josephine, even then. It isn't about your looks. It's you. The whole package."

"What if... what happens when I die?" she asked, looking over at me, eyes sad.

"You've seen Minos," I told her. "Something like that. Something would always feel like it was missing if you weren't here."

Her eyes looked a bit glassy at that.

Not for herself.

For the pain a future version of myself might feel.

"What if... what if I didn't want to die?"

"You can't make that decision."

"It's my life. Mortal or not," she insisted, those tears vanishing. Her chin lifted; her spine straightened. I liked her soft and sweet, but her headstrong and defiant was sexy as fuck.

"Fine," I said, giving her a small smile, trailing a finger down her tight jaw. "You can't make that decision *right now*," I told her. "We can revisit it in a while if you decide your feelings aren't going to change."

I could tell she didn't like that answer, but the rational part of her had to admit there was merit to my suggestion.

"I guess I can live with that," she agreed.

"And me?" I asked. "At least for now?" I qualified.

"I think that can be arranged," she said, giving me a smile before climbing on my lap, sealing her lips over mine.

True, I might one day have to confront the idea of her no longer choosing me.

But right then, right that moment, she was choosing me.

And that was all that mattered.

Epilogue

Jo - 1 Day

He had wings.

I mean, objectively, I'd known that.

Changed fully into his True Form, he had wings. But from what I could tell, it almost never happened on the human plane. Except, of course, when you Claimed someone. Like Ly and done with Lenore.

But Ace had wings.

They were the loveliest and most incredible things I had ever seen.

I thought maybe they were all the same. Black and bat-like. Mostly because that was what Ly's were like and I had no other frame of reference.

But Ace's wings were different. Yes, they were bat-like. And, yes, they were predominantly black. But there was another color dotted in, almost like glitter. A brilliant, lovely golden color that I couldn't stop staring at, so I was glad that Ace seemed to have trouble tucking them back away now that they were out.

They were all kinds of sexy and soothing when they brushed over my bare skin, too, which added an interesting new element to sex later the night of the Claiming. And the next morning.

I guess it shouldn't have been so fascinating, so charming.

I probably should have run screaming.

They were evil.

He was evil.

And yet... and yet, somehow, I'd seen more kindness in him than I had in many humans with their supposed souls.

He was fiercely loyal to his club, his people. He had worried himself sick over Red. He'd sat up with her every night to read to her.

When he'd taken me out for the day, I don't think he realized I noticed his very sly handoff of a handful of cash to a homeless man sitting out front of the convenience store beside the pizza place we'd gone to.

Not just his spare change or a dollar or something.

When I'd glanced back, the bill that was wrapped around several other bills was a fifty.

He might have shown outright derision for humans at times, but there was no denying he'd developed a certain softness toward some of us. The downtrodden, the ones our society never looked twice at, the souls that likely would ascend, not end up down in hell getting tormented for eternity.

When we talked about things he'd seen and experienced since coming to Earth, he'd raged about how humans set themselves apart in groups, about how their fear and petty prejudices were the dark marks on their souls that would send them down instead of up.

He didn't like Earth-side suffering.

He didn't like seeing division based on race and sexuality and politics.

He'd waxed poetic about how, as a whole, humans had evolved immensely with terms of technology, but almost not at all about things that really mattered.

You didn't even want to get him *started* on religion. Because at the end of the day, in his words, 'Good is good and evil is evil and everyone knows what is good and what is evil, but pretend that only they know, so they can hate each other, and start wars, and do the exact opposite of what is good.'

For an immortal being, he was surprisingly "up on the times." Or "woke," if you will.

And for a creature that was, well, evil, he liked to see people being good, people ascending. Even though he whispered in the ears of others to bring out their evil.

When I'd maybe called him a hypocrite for that, he'd rolled his eyes at me. "You can't make a good person evil, Josephine. It is there or it isn't. We just tease it out when it is there."

I'd even asked him to try it on me. And even after a lot of suggesting, I'd just been sleepy.

So I was good.

Which left me in a tough spot, didn't it?

Because if I wanted to be with Ace in a forever sort of way, I would have to become less good. Not fully evil. Lenore was still partly good, partly human. Or, well, witch. Which I think still made her human. I'd been so wrapped up with demon lore that I hadn't gotten my crash course on witches yet. But it was coming, I was sure.

So if I decided to let Lenore make me immortal as well, I would still be myself. But I would live forever. I wouldn't be so bothered by more pesky human things. Like eating. Like pain.

But in order to have those things happen, some of my soul wouldn't be around anymore.

It was a big thing to contemplate, something weighty, something I wasn't ready to decide yet, like Ace had suggested.

Yes, I was borderline obsessed with Ace at this point, but I knew enough about hormones to know that oxytocin, dopamine, and serotonin were wreaking havoc on my system, making it hard to know my mind from my heart and the other way around.

I needed time.

To make sure it wasn't just chemical infatuation.

I had to say, though, I already knew it was more than that. Because I genuinely liked Ace. Snarky asshole side and all. Because while he was that, he would always be that, with me, he was something else. He was softer, sweeter, and kinder. And I knew that because of his nature, he would always be those things toward me.

I also had a lot of respect for his loyalty to his people, his steadfast determination to lead them, to guide them as the world changed around them constantly. I adored his thirst for knowledge, even if it sometimes made him come off a little cocky and condescending. Usually it turned me off when people thought they knew more than you. But in this case, it was a simple fact. The man had been around ages. He'd read millions of books. He'd seen and done it all.

And he liked sharing that knowledge. He enjoyed telling me things, giving me the knowledge he'd acquired over his very long life. It was almost like he felt like he was giving me pieces of himself by doing so. Luckily, I was hungry for all things supernatural or paranormal or whatever it was called. I was sure I would never get enough of his stories.

So, yeah, there were chemicals involved, but there was genuine affection as well.

And we would just have to see where all of that would lead us.

Ace - 1 Month

The party felt different than all the previous ones.

And there had been many of them.

I guess the difference could be attributed to the woman who had been moving around the house during it. The one in a skintight black dress she'd borrowed from Red who still hadn't come home to reclaim her closet that made me both want to grab her, wrap my wing—or just my fucking coat—around her so no one else could see, but also shove up against a wall, slip up the skirt, and fuck her right there for everyone to see that she—and all those curves that were coming back thanks to our twice-weekly fast food binge trips—belonged to me.

She made the party different, my work different.

She made everything different.

I knew, on a rational level, that should have bothered me.

But I couldn't seem to give a fuck.

Because I'd been on Earth for a long, long time, and I'd never come close to anything resembling happiness as I did since she came into my life.

It was warm.

She was warm.

She was the kind of warm I'd been chasing since I'd left hell.

She was the kind of warm I would give up going back there for.

Just to stay here, basking in it.

Forever.

Or for as long as she would let me have it.

That thought made my mood darker and darker as the days dragged to weeks. Because the more of her I got, the more I wanted, the less I felt like letting her go even if she demanded it of me.

Eventually, I'd decided to abandon the party early, leaving the fun and games to the other guys while

I tossed my woman over my shoulder, threw her on the bed, and gave her half a dozen orgasms until she couldn't take anymore.

But the party had been over for hours.

And there was the sound of voices below.

Hushed voices.

But rapid, angry, even.

An argument of some sort.

Sure, it could have been Ly and Lenore, but I rarely ever heard them fighting.

It could even have been one of Daemon's many women, angry at being kicked out.

But something told me to get out of bed, put on some pants, and go down to check things out.

I was halfway down the stairs when I'd found the source of the male voice.

Not Ly or Daemon.

And the woman's voice.

Not Lenore or some random clubwhore.

Oh, no.

Nope.

This was Dale.

Dale the fucking demon*slayer*.

"What the fuck are you doing here?" I snapped before I could fully assess the situation.

And it was right then and there that I realized something vital.

Because Minos's wings surged out from his back, moving over to attempt to wrap protectively around Dale.

Who visibly shrank away, casting an angry look at Minos, and a guilty one at me, before turning, yanking open the door, and disappearing.

I wasn't sure what I was supposed to feel at realizing one of my men had Claimed a demonslayer.

But the sigh that moved through me felt appropriate.

As well as the words that came out of my mouth.

"Are you fucking serious?"

To that, Minos's jaw went tight as his wings disappeared.

"I think we both know we don't have any control over it," he snapped, jaw tight.

With that, he stormed off, slamming the back door as he went outside.

Leaving me to contemplate all the ways this shit could come back and bite us in the ass.

I don't know how long I stood there.

But I knew it was Josephine's hands that snapped me out of my swirling thoughts as they slid around my chest. She leaned forward, resting her head against my bare back.

"Come back to bed," she demanded in a sleepy voice.

So, no, I had no fucking idea what it meant that Minos had claimed Dale.

I didn't have any idea where Red was, or why she was chasing down Marceaus who didn't seem like he wanted to be caught.

I didn't even know what it meant for us that Drex was so obsessed with his kinky fucking club.

But I did know I was going back to bed with my woman.

And in that moment, it was all that mattered.

Jo - 1 Year

"Are you sure?" Lenore asked, tone serious.

Because she knew what a big decision this was.

She'd needed to make it as well.

"You've been where I'm standing," I reminded her. "You know the answer to that."

I hadn't taken the decision lightly.

I figured she hadn't either.

It was a big thing, asking someone to give up what they had always known.

Birth, life, death.

A cycle that never had an opt-out clause before.

We'd molded our lives as such, made decisions based on the need to experience as much as we could in such a short time, knowing it would soon all be over.

It was a big deal to suddenly decide that was no longer going to be your reality. I'd spent many sleepless nights wrestling with my uncertainties about it. I'd pestered Lenore endlessly about the differences she'd felt after she'd taken on immortality.

I was afraid things would lose their wonder because I knew I would always have them, that no moment was lost because I would have infinite chances to experience the same thing over and over. I was terrified to lose my sense of purpose, something that had always been so important to me.

Unexpectedly, it had been Drex to calm that particular worry. Granted, he'd done so gruffly and with a voice full of annoyance over listening to me prattle on endlessly about it to Ace.

"Wouldn't being alive forever give you more chances to help the hurt and infirm, for fuck's sake?"

And, well, he was right.

Maybe I couldn't do it at my old capacity. People would eventually notice that I wasn't aging. But I could still help. I could find purpose.

After four or five months, when the feelings toward Ace hadn't started to ebb, but just flowed endlessly, I figured my worries about it being chemical were pretty unfounded.

It was just him.

I liked him.

No.

I *loved* him.

I loved him in a way I never had before.

Suddenly, I could see the shallowness in all my previous relationships.

I'd loved conditionally.

And I'd been loved back the same way.

There was none of that with Ace and me.

He loved me without limits.

I loved him without fear.

It was thrilling and terrifying and so consuming it was hard to wrap my own head around at times. And I was the one experiencing it.

All I knew was, each day, I became more and more certain that what I wanted, what I needed, was more time with him.

As much time as I could possibly have.

"I know," Lenore agreed, looking up from the grimoire in her hands. "I just have to check," she added, giving me a soft smile. "It's a big decision."

"The biggest," I agreed.

"It's the best one I've ever made," she told me in a low voice, not wanting our men to overhear.

"I know it is going to be the best one I ever have too," I assured her, feeling Ace's wing tickle across my neck as he moved forward, came to stand behind me. Always having my back. Especially during such an important moment.

With that, Lenore started her spell.

I said the words she told me to say.

And my whole heart was in my voice as I did so.

Because that was what Ace was going to have.

Forever.

Sneak Peek!

The front door flew open.
Footsteps rushed into the library.
And there was Daemon, wide-eyed, out of breath.
"Hey, ah, boss man," he said, looking over at Ace. "I, uhm, I think Drex might have just gotten us into a war with the vampires. Just thought you'd want to know that."

Also By Jessica Gadziala

If you liked this book, check out these other series and titles in the NAVESINK BANK UNIVERSE:

The Henchmen MC
Reign
Cash
Wolf
Repo
Duke
Renny
Lazarus
Pagan
Cyrus
Edison
Reeve
Sugar
The Fall of V

Adler
Roderick
Virgin
Roan
Camden
West
Colson

The Henchmen MC - Next Gen
Niro

The Savages
Monster
Killer
Savior

Mallick Brothers
For A Good Time, Call
Shane
Ryan
Mark
Eli
Charlie & Helen: Back to the Beginning

Investigators
367 Days
14 Weeks
4 Months

Dark
Dark Mysteries
Dark Secrets

Dark Horse

Professionals
The Fixer
The Ghost
The Messenger
The General
The Babysitter
The Negotiator
The Client

Rivers Brothers
Lift You Up
Lock You Down
Pull You In

STANDALONES WITHIN NAVESINK BANK:
Vigilante
Grudge Match
The Rise of Ferryn
Counterfeit Love

Golden Glades Henchmen
Huck

OTHER SERIES AND STANDALONES

Stars Landing
What The Heart Needs
What The Heart Wants
What The Heart Finds

What The Heart Knows
The Stars Landing Deviant
What The Heart Learns

Surrogate
The Sex Surrogate
Dr. Chase Hudson

The Green Series
Into the Green
Escape from the Green

DEBT
Dissent
Stuffed: A Thanksgiving Romance
There Better Be Pie
Unwrapped
Peace, Love, & Macarons
A Navesink Bank Christmas
Don't Come
Fix It Up
N.Y.E.
faire l'amour
The Woman at the Docks
The Woman in the Trunk
The Sacrifice
Ugly Sweater Weather

About the Author

Jessica Gadziala is a full-time writer, parrot enthusiast, and coffee drinker who enjoys short rides to the bookstore, sad songs, and cold weather, and who has developed an unhealthy obsession with acquiring houseplants. She lives in New Jersey with a bunch of dogs, seven parrots, and a whole flock of chickens.

She is a strong believer in snark, strong secondary characters, and badass women.

Stalk Her!

Connect with Jessica:

Facebook:
https://www.facebook.com/JessicaGadziala/
Facebook Group:
https://www.facebook.com/groups/314540025563403/

Goodreads:
https://www.goodreads.com/author/show/13800950.Jessica_Gadziala
Goodreads Group:
https://www.goodreads.com/group/show/177944-jessica-gadziala-books-and-bullsh

Twitter: @JessicaGadziala

JessicaGadziala.com

www.ingramcontent.com/pod-product-compliance
Lightning Source LLC
Chambersburg PA
CBHW020329160726
47992CB00004B/1772